A SMOKY LITTLE Christmas

SunflowerROSE
PUBLISHING

Cover Design by Jared Roach at DRMR Creative

Editing by: Tylee Hardman at Markd by Tylee

For anyone who still believes that Christmas magic shows up exactly when we need it the most.

Chapter One
Monae

"For the last time, I am not taking this thing!" I huffed, pushing the old journal back toward my friend Brina who kept trying to slip it into my bag when she thought I wasn't looking.

Brina sighed and shoved it into my bag once more. "But it has your name in it! I can't just ignore that, who knows what will happen?"

The five of us: Elodie, Audrey, Brina, Deja, and me were all sitting in Elodie's living room sorting through the various designs she had picked out. She was due to marry her fiancé Mekhi in the next year, after being engaged for nearly two. She gave herself a year to just bask in being engaged and now the wedding planning was in full swing, set for the Christmas season of next year. Gave me plenty of time to stuff myself into the backless, silver sequined dress she requested all of her bridesmaids wear.

"God, forbid we upset the Almighty Journal." I scoffed, rolling my eyes.

I'd seen the mysterious book in action three times before. The first time was when Elodie received it as a gift from her grandmother, Amada, who told her that she'd received it from her grandmother Noel. The second time I saw it happen, was when Elodie gave it to Audrey and then the third time was when Audrey gave it to Brina. Each time, the journal had a knack for gently pushing them in the direction of their happily ever after. Supposedly. I'd seen the pages flip on their own and the words mysteriously appear as if a ghost had sat down to tell a story, so I couldn't deny that there was some validity to its claims. Still, I had no interest in being its next victim.

I saw how obsessive it made my girls when the entries would appear overnight, sometimes immediately after they interacted with their potential matches. They'd ignore the common sense they were born with and default to what the journal was encouraging them to do. To me, it didn't seem like a fun time. The idea of putting my future into the hands of a crusty old book seemed absurd.

"This thing is like a chain letter, and you're not about to give me bad luck for seven years by not taking it." Brina folded her arms and glared at me, even though there was a hint of a smile on her lips.

"Fine. But I reserve the right to protest if I don't like who it matches me with."

"Fair enough. So, El, do you have a venue in mind yet?" Brina leaned back on the couch and tilted her head up to look at Elodie, who was standing directly behind her with her nose in her phone, typing furiously.

"Hmm?" she replied, absentmindedly.

"Venue, love." Brina repeated.

"Right! Yes. The Iron Library on 5th and Connor. My desired date opened up recently, so I jumped on it." She locked her phone and put it back in her pocket.

I shook my head, not at all surprised that she'd pick that library. She'd met her favorite author, Anya James, over there after Anya had published the book about her parents Henry and Clara's miraculous love story. It was a quaint library, not as well-known unless you were a local, but it was full of culture and beautiful displays. It'd make for some gorgeous wedding photos.

"As your Maid of Honor," Audrey began, a mischievous grin spreading across her face, "I call dibs on planning the bachelorette weekend."

Deja perked up from her spot in the armchair directly across from the couch, "Excuse me? I called dibs on that last year. I've already been planning. There are strippers involved. Don't take this away from me!"

"We'll talk." Audrey replied. Deja narrowed her eyes.

"Hey, Dej," I said, waving the journal in her direction, "Don't you want to take my turn with this thing?"

"Absolutely not," she replied, "Unless it can promise me a man with a big dick and an even bigger bank account, I'm good love, enjoy."

"How romantic." Elodie rolled her eyes, a smile tugging at the corners of her mouth. I snorted at her comment, leave it to Deja to say something completely off the wall. Even though she had a point, the big dick wasn't necessarily a requirement, but well established would be nice. Definitely not in the business of building up a man based on potential. Come fully potenched, please.

"When is the next book club meeting? And what are we even reading?" I asked, pulling up my StoryGraph account and scrolling through some of the past choices we had. A few of them I loved and some of them weren't that great to me, but I was always grateful for the motivation to read. If it wasn't for my girls and the Novel-Tea book club we started back in college, I probably would have shoved reading on the back burner. Especially reading for fun. It's so easy to let other things take precedence. My job had its demanding and sometimes dangerous moments, even if it mostly felt like living in a slightly more professional frat house most days. I had to make it a point to find time to read and actively fight against letting work consume me.

"We can try that new Kennedy Ryan book." Elodie offered with a slight shrug of her rapidly slimming shoulders. In her desire to fit into her wedding dress, she had been hitting the gym with Audrey and I quite often. After her initial complaining, she started to see the fun in weightlifting. I needed to do it to keep up with the demands of my job, but there was comfort in it as well. "I think it's called Can't Get Enough."

"I already read that one." Brina winced when we all whipped around to stare at her. "What? Langston knows her publisher. He was able to get me an advanced copy before the release date a while back."

"How does it feel to be God's favorite?" I grumbled, as my phone vibrating in my pocket caught my attention. I slipped it out and glanced down at the message.

Brown, can you spot me my portion on the groceries tonight? I got you next payday.

I rolled my eyes at the message from Eugene Branch, one of the firefighters frequently on shift with me. He felt more like an annoying little brother than a coworker. We got close when he was a probie and I had been on the crew for a few years.

You said that last time. Not a chance.

I replied and stuffed the phone back in my pocket. I wasn't on the clock until tomorrow morning, but it wasn't unheard of for him to text me asking to cover his part of the groceries. I was starting to think he emptied his bank account into the fires whenever we had a call. He never had any money.

"Can we read a book about marriage?" Elodie asked. I looked up from my phone just in time to see the look of disgust cross over Deja's face. She caught my eye, and I flashed her a look of my own.

"Girl." I laughed. "We know you got it bad for Mekhi, but please don't make us singles suffer even more than we need to."

"Well, it's your turn with the journal." Brina said. "So, you won't be single for much longer."

"Exactly!" Audrey chimed in from her spot at the counter, fixing snacks for all of us to enjoy.

I turned back to Deja and groaned, "Dej, you're the only one left with some sense. Please help me."

She threw her hands up in mock surrender, "We don't stand a chance against these lovesick losers, Mon. Don't fight it, just go limp."

The five of us laughed as Audrey brought the tray of food in and we settled into our usual places in the living room. We'd spent so much time at each other's houses and apartments over the years; it was no wonder there wasn't a permanent indentation in the shape of my butt on this recliner.

"The next book club meeting is in about two weeks." Brina said, checking her calendar. "Any ideas of what book we want to tackle? Something short preferably, I've got a heavy caseload these next few months."

While we sat around in a circle munching on the snacks Audrey had prepared and debating on what book to read next, my mind drifted away from the conversation and back to the journal that was already burning a hole in my bag. Did I believe in the magic of it? I'd technically seen it work a few times, but I wasn't sure that was enough to sway my opinion. Elodie, Brina, and Audrey were all excited about the possibilities and who the journal would encourage me to match with, but it was going to take more than a few self-flipping pages to really get me on their side.

The next morning, I popped my eyes open with a groan. I'd had a few too many margaritas last night with the girls and my head was pounding. Twenty-year-old me would have been able to knock back multiple drinks and pop up later like nothing happened, but now that I w firmly in my thirties, the snap-back took a little

more time

Blazme. blue-nosed Pitbull, jumped on the bed and glared

I was ten minutes late for his morning walk and he

dot pleased. I had about five minutes to get up and get him

ide before he decided to make one of my shoes his toilet as

unishment.

"I'm coming, Blazey boy," I said, rubbing his block head. "Just give me a second." He huffed in the way that only he knows how to and left the room to curl up on the couch while he waited. I had four minutes and fifty-nine seconds. Logically, I knew he couldn't tell time, but in moments like these it felt like he could.

I got myself together and took Blaze out right in the nick of time. He grumbled the entire walk as a result. My grumpy old man. I'd gotten him a few years after my girls had each gotten their dogs. I hadn't planned to adopt, with my schedule causing me to be away from home a lot, but an automatic feeder and one of my girls coming over while I was at work to let him out, helped make sure he got what he needed. When I saw his grumpy face glaring at the camera on the adoption page I followed on Facebook, I couldn't resist bringing him home.

By the time I made it to the station, I was two cups of coffee and three Tylenol in. That was the last time I'd let Brina mix drinks when I was supposed to go into work the next day. She had a heavy hand and the alcohol tolerance of a much larger man.

"Brown! It's about time you showed up." Sean Pittman called out, clapping me on the back, "It's your turn to clean the toilets today and I had some really sketchy Mexican food last night." He rubbed his stomach with his free hand and let out a loud, sn~~ly belch. My~~ stomach curled in disgust.

"I swear you do this on purpose." I grumbled, rolling
Sean was another one that felt more like a brother than a cowes.
even though he always managed to find my last nerve and sto.
on it with both feet. He was full of jokes and childish behavior or.
a regular basis, but when it came down to responding to a call—
especially the hard ones—there is no one else I'd rather have with
me. He would protect me and watch my back at all costs, which was
important in calls where surprises were likely to happen.

"Love you too." He laughed. "You good? You're looking a little
green around the gills."

"I'm good." I replied, heading towards our makeshift locker
room to put my things down. Sean trailed behind me, chattering
happily about his girlfriend and how she was ready for him to meet
her parents over the holiday season. I listened quietly as he talked,
chiming in every so often with a 'mhm' and 'oh okay that's dope' so
he could keep going. Sean was really into this new girl, which was
a first for him.

He'd been the playboy of the shift until Layla, a girl who was
stuck in her house during a fire after a faulty smoke detector failed
to let her know, swooped in and knocked him off his feet. You'd
think it'd be the other way around, since he was the one to get her
out of her house safely, but he was smitten from the moment he
saw her. A hallmark movie in the making if I'd ever heard one.

I reached down into my bookbag, my fingers curling around the
journal that Brina had insisted I kept on me at all times. I don't
know why I listened, maybe it was because I felt like she would

somehow be able to tell if I didn't. The last thing I wanted was Brina pinning me with her lawyer stare and fussing at me. She could be scary when she wanted.

"What is that?" Sean asked, peering over my shoulder at the journal, "You taking up writing in your spare time?"

"Something like that." I mumbled. I wasn't about to explain to him what the purpose of this dusty book was. It'd be spread across the fire station by the end of the shift, and I would never hear the end of it.

"Anyway, Chief Lillard wants us to line up in a few. Probably wants to give us the holiday schedule for this year. I'm going to go take another caca real quick beforehand." I rolled my eyes in disgust as Sean wiggled his eyebrows and backed out of the locker room. I didn't even want to think about the crimes he would commit in there and then leave for me to clean up.

As soon as I was alone in the room, I heard a quiet rustling behind me. I turned, expecting to find a window open, only to see the journal I had placed on the bench in front of my locker opened and flipping its pages on its own. I stared, dumbfounded. This was happening early, I didn't expect anything to start until much later. Brina, Audrey, and Elodie had mentioned that the journal usually did its thing in the middle of the night. Now here we are, first thing in the morning, and the pages were flipping back and forth like some special effect in an action movie.

"Brown!" a voice bellowed, distracting me from the journal. "It's time for lineup!"

I hesitated, debating whether I wanted to read the journal first and then go to lineup even though I knew better than that. Whenever the Chief called for a lineup, we had five seconds to stop what we were doing and get out there or it would be hell to pay. The captain was the one that usually called, so when the boss's boss requests something, that has to be respected. I sighed and closed the journal. I'd get to it after lineup.

I made it downstairs and into the room right as the Chief turned the corner and faced us. He was an older gentleman, having been in the field for years after climbing his way up the ranks. He was broad shouldered, tall, with a salt and pepper beard over smooth chocolate skin and eyes that were kind but stern. Even though he had been happily married for decades now, women still threw themselves at him whenever he was out in the community. It was comical to watch him sidestep the advances of women in all age ranges.

"Team, I've volunteered the station to help with the Christmas festivities at Whispering Pines Nursing Home this year." He began, "My mother is currently stationed there and I want to make sure she has some extra Christmas joy this year. I've already decided which ones of you will be helping out over there and which ones will stay here to man the station."

I crossed my fingers, hoping I'd be one of those chosen to stick around the station to make sure everything went okay here. As much as I loved Christmas and volunteering with the community, the nursing home is the last place I wanted to be. No offense to them or anything, but those places had an air of death about them that made me uncomfortable. Like people just dumped their older family members there when they became too much of a liability. The few times I'd been at a nursing home, I could feel the vibes of the place sucking the energy out of me. I'd prefer to stay at the station, even if that meant taking on extra work while team members were unavailable.

"Pittman, Branch, Arnold, Normil, and Daniels, you will be working with Whispering Pines." Chief looked at each of them individually while I resisted the urge to pump my fist in the air after not hearing my name called. "And Brown. You'll go to supervise. Can't leave these knuckleheads to their own devices without someone there to watch over them."

My heart sank, but I nodded anyway. "Sure thing, Chief."

"The rest of you will stay here and answer calls as they come. Everyone get back to work. Whispering Pines crew, stay behind please." I watched sullenly as the ones chosen to stay behind filed out of the room one by one. The only good thing about it, I wouldn't have to clean the toilets like I thought. Whatever nonsense Sean left in there would be someone else's problem.

"Whispering Pines Nursing Home is having a weekly Christmas event for the month of December in order to engage their residents in the holiday season and spread some cheer." He handed each of us a sheet of paper. It was a list of the activities we would be helping with once per week. The final activity was a big dinner for the fire station, the nursing home residents and their invited family members.

Food will be provided at each event, and it would be catered by The Hungry Hippo. I smiled at the name of the restaurant. That was Montrell's place. The same restaurant that was the source of my girl Audrey's misery two years ago but now an integral part of her business, Audrey's Kitchen. If the two restaurant owners hadn't connected during their cooking competition, who knows where Audrey and Montrell would be now.

I briefly considered Jai Carter, Montrell's business partner. I'd seen him at the competition and a few times when hanging out afterwards, but I couldn't take him seriously. He was attractive, deep brown skin with sharply lined facial hair and eyes that can pull you into his aura like a moth to a flame, but he seemed so goofy and awkward. Like he always needed to be the center of attention and didn't feel comfortable if he wasn't being the class clown. There was nothing wrong with a sense of humor, but sometimes things require you to be serious.

It was an interesting dynamic between Jai, Montrell, and Audrey as they bounced ideas off of each other to generate more business for each of their restaurants. I'd attended a few events they threw to show my support. Maybe this wouldn't be so bad this time. At least I could count on some good food to hold me over until it was time to head out.

The first event would be tree decorating. That couldn't be all that difficult, could it? We were instructed to make some simple, homemade ornaments and then help the residents decorate the two trees in their communal dining room. We'd need to make a quick stop at a craft store before we went, but none of the ornaments required anything too serious.

I headed back to the locker room to grab my stuff, resigned to the fact that I would be entertaining the elderly for this shift. The journal was poking out of my bag from where I hastily shoved it in earlier. There was an entry waiting for me that I still hadn't read yet. The idea of reading what it said suddenly made me nervous. What if it tried to match me with one of the guys at the station? The idea made my face scrunch in disgust. If that crusty journal thought it would convince me to make things romantic with any of the guys here, I was going to rip it apart page by page and mail them back to Elodie, Brina, and Audrey one by one.

"Who wants to drive to this place?" Sean called out. "I need gas in my truck, but we can take it."

"I'll meet you guys there. I have to make a quick stop first." I said over my shoulder as I made my way back to my car. If I was going to read this entry, I wanted privacy. The last thing I needed was one of the guys looking over my shoulder at anything this journal said. I settled into the drivers' seat and turned on the car. The heat blasted against my face, instantly warming it from the two minutes it took to get from the front door to my vehicle.

In the privacy of my car, with the heat blasting and Leon Thomas's latest album playing, I reached into my bag and pulled out the journal. The edges were slightly curled, letting me know that this journal had seen better days.

"Alright," I sighed, "Here goes nothing." I opened the journal and flipped to the one page with writing.

DEAR DIARY,

SHE'S ALWAYS LOOKED FOR SPARKS IN THE OBVIOUS PLACES. SHE LOOKS FOR THE LOUD GESTURES, PERFECT TIMING, THE MEN WHO CHECKED ALL THE BOXES. BUT LOVE, REAL LOVE, DOESN'T ALWAYS ARRIVE IN A BLAZE. SOMETIMES IT SMOLDERS IN SILENCE, WAITING TO BE SEEN.

THIS TIME, SHE MUST LET GO OF HER CHECKLIST AND LOOK AGAIN. NOT WITH HER EYES, BUT WITH HER HEART. THE ONE SHE'S LEAST EXPECTED HAS ALREADY NOTICED HER. WILL SHE BE BRAVE ENOUGH TO NOTICE HIM BACK? IT BEGINS, NOT WITH ?REWORKS, BUT WITH BURNT COOKIES AND CROOKED SMILES. IF SHE

PAYS ATTENTION, SHE'LL REALIZE: THE ONE SHE NEVER CONSIDERED MIGHT BE EXACTLY WHO SHE'S BEEN WAITING FOR.

I stared at the words, allowing confusion and a little disappointment to wash over me. In the past, it was vocal with Brina, Audrey, and Elodie. It literally told them by name who they should keep their eye out for, but with me it was vague. No names. No hints. Nothing that I could use to keep an eye out for this mystery man that was supposed to have already noticed me.

"But love, real love, doesn't always arrive in a blaze. Sometimes it smolders in the silence, waiting to be seen. Real heavy on the fire puns, I see." I whispered to myself, trying to wrack my brain for an idea.

A sharp knock on my window made me jump out of my skin. I closed the journal with a snap and turned to find Sean pressed against my window, a silly grin spreading across his already flushed face.

"What are you doing in there, Brown?" he called, his voice muffled through the window. "Now is not the time to be writing about your feelings!"

"What do you want?" I asked.

"Can I ride with you? Don't feel like using my gas."

I rolled my eyes, "Get in."

As he raced to the other side of my car, I tucked the journal under my seat. I had no idea who it was trying to nudge me toward, but I didn't have time to think about that now. I could mull over it later after we finished at Whispering Pines. Maybe I could call my girls and try to figure out what this thing was trying to get me to see. Either way, for now, this Christmas love story could wait.

Chapter Two

Jai

"Jai!" Montrell called from the kitchen. "Why am I getting voicemails from Whispering Pines saying you've volunteered the restaurant to cater their Christmas events for free?"

I flinched. I'd been hoping to come up with a plan to get Montrell onboard before the nursing home called to confirm, but it looks like their administrative assistant is more thorough than I anticipated. I got the idea from a friend of mine who works at the nursing home. She mentioned that the local fire station, Willow Glen, would be volunteering with the residents of Whispering Pines over the next few weeks.

Willow Glen Fire Station or Station 4 for short, meant...her. Monae. The object of my desires for the last few years, even though she hasn't done so much as spared me a passing glance. Ever since that cooking competition that Montrell and his current girlfriend Audrey competed in, Monae was all I could think about. She had a vibe that commanded my attention, not through spectacle or through force, but through a presence that was so self-assured it felt like the gravity around me shifted to make space for her. Her smooth espresso skin that glowed against the ugly fluorescent lights of the filming studio and her long dark hair that hung over her shoulders drew me in immediately. I noticed her angular cheek bones and soft almond eyes that scanned the room when she didn't think anyone was watching. I was watching. I couldn't help it. She was the type that listened more than she talked, but when she did speak, every word was intentional. Her look was simple, yet elegant and enough to mentally knock me to my knees.

I'd been trying to catch her eye ever since, and while she has always been polite, I haven't been able to get any deeper than surface level. She'd respond when I approached her and laugh politely at my jokes, but it always felt like she was looking through me; never at me. And I vowed that this year would be the year I changed that.

When Ariella told me the fire station Monae worked for would be volunteering with the nursing home residents this year, I blurted out that The Hungry Hippo would be more than happy to cater. For free. Without checking to see if the man behind the spatula, Montrell, would even be willing to take on such a project. Oops.

"Oh, right!" I began, "I may have signed us up to cater the nursing home this year." I entered the kitchen and tried my best not to wither under his stare. If I could talk him into it, all would be well—but judging from the look on his face, that would be a lot harder than I thought.

"Us? Since when do you cook?" He folded his arms and glared at me.

"I mean, we are a team, are we not?"

"Jai-"

"I know I know, before you start complaining, just hear me out." He narrowed his eyes and waited. I combed through all of the excuses I had lined up, but nothing felt right. I sighed and then my shoulders sagged in defeat. "Willow Glen Station is volunteering."

Montrell's expression softened slightly, "As in... Monae's station?"

I nodded. "Yeah. Ariella told me the station is helping with some of the events for their residents this holiday season and I couldn't resist."

"You've been trying to get her attention for years now. What makes you think it'll work this time?"

"I don't know," I shrugged, "something feels different this time. My gut is telling me it's now or never."

I couldn't put my finger on why, but it felt like if I finally decided to shoot my shot, it would be received well this time. She'd given me no indication that she was interested in me at all, but my gut was finally telling me to go for it. If there was one thing that I always listened to, it was my gut. It was what convinced me to do things like go into business with Montrell and enter him into a Christmas themed cooking competition that ended up generating so much business for us, we were considering opening a new location.

"Why do your gut feelings always result in more work for me?" He folded his arms across his chest and narrowed his eyes at me.

"Name one time it didn't end up being beneficial." I shot back. "I recall a cooking competition that was the catalyst for us opening a new location across town and connected you with the love of your life. You're welcome by the way."

Montrell sighed and shook his head. He was pushing back on the idea at the moment, but this was our usual dynamic. I pitch an idea; he pitches a fit and then we hash it out and move forward with my idea. All I had to do was wait for him to complain about it a little more and then he'd be on my side.

"Fine. If this works, maybe she can calm you down some." he grumbled. "Give me a moment of peace for once."

"That'll never happen. Anyway, I've compiled a list of the easier meals on our menu that can be prepped ahead of time. They're grabbing sandwiches from the sandwich shop down the street for today, but tomorrow will be some of the food inspired events, so we'll need to-"

Montrell held up a hand to silence me, "We? Absolutely not. I will prep the food, but it's on you to deliver it and make sure it's ready for the residents."

"You said yourself that I don't cook. Why leave me out there to fail like that?"

"I need to insert boundaries somewhere." He chuckled. "I haven't forgotten when I was forced to wear a glittery Santa hat because of you. I was finding glitter everywhere for months afterwards."

Montrell was subjected to a lot of silly Christmas behavior during that competition, including a host that looked like he stepped straight off the set of Willy Wonka so I couldn't blame him for trying to remove himself from the line of fire this time. If we prepped simple foods, I could represent The Hungry Hippo with enough ease to make it seem like I could cook. Hopefully, Monae wouldn't notice.

"Fine. At least show me how to do some of it." Montrell nodded and motioned for me to follow him into the kitchen. A quick crash course in meal prep couldn't hurt, but at this point, I wasn't sure it would help either.

"The tree decorating is the first event." I looked down at the information I had hastily scribbled after talking to the administrative assistant for Whispering Pines. From what I could read of my handwriting, today would be decorating the tree, next would be an ugly sweater event, a Christmas treat event and then a final Christmas dinner where the residents were free to invite their friends and family.

After a few rounds of arguing, I managed to get Montrell to agree to helping with the final Christmas dinner. I'm pretty sure the only reason he agreed was so my lack of cooking skills wouldn't completely tarnish our restaurant's reputation. Couldn't say I blamed him.

I didn't need to be here for this first event, but I wanted an excuse to see Monae. I figured I could show up with snacks and pretend that I didn't realize they wouldn't need me until next week. Hopefully she wouldn't see through my act.

By the time I arrived at Whispering Pines, it was early afternoon. According to Ariella, they were due to start decorating in about an hour. I entered the front lobby and scanned the room for someone that could help me. Residents roamed the hallways in varying degrees of coherence. A few sat in a group to my left playing cards in what looked to be a recreation room, while others hovered near the railings on the hallway walls.

"Hi. I'm Jasmine. Can I help you?" A young girl with a long braid down her back came bounding towards me at alarming speed.

"I'm here for the Christmas event. With Willow Glen."

I watched as her pleasant expression morphed into one of skepticism. She looked me up and down, studying my appearance with narrowed eyes.

"You're...a firefighter?" She asked, disbelief heavy in her voice.

"No. I'm Jai Carter, with The Hungry Hippo. The restaurant that was hired to cater."

"Oh. That makes more sense!" It was my turn to narrow my eyes. I wasn't the most muscular individual, but I am in decent shape. For the most part. I don't turn down dessert, but I can still run a mile on the treadmill. Maybe. Depends on the circumstances. "They're getting set up in the dining hall. Come with me, I'll show you."

I followed behind her as she bounded down the hall, greeting some of the residents as she went. She didn't look a day over eighteen, but I couldn't be too sure. We made our way down the hall and turned a corner on the right. The typical smells of a nursing home, antiseptic and stale skin, got stronger the further into the building we went. It wasn't enough to turn my stomach, but it wasn't a pleasant smell.

The walls of the nursing home were plain, hospital white aside from the occasional board nailed to the wall with old flyers and nursing shifts. The vibe of the entire building was heavy and depressing. So many of the residents were brought here and left by their families who no longer had the time, patience, or resources to care for them. The place felt like a museum of lost memories doomed to waste away in these tiny rooms with the tiny beds.

It made this Christmas event that Willow Glen and Hungry Hippo were helping with feel that much more special. This would probably be the only type of holiday celebration many of them would receive. I vowed in that moment to make sure it was enjoyable for as many people as possible. By any means necessary. Monae was my primary mission, but a secondary mission for Christmas joy couldn't hurt.

"Here we are! A few people are in here setting up already. I guess you can go right in." Jasmine gestured toward the dining hall over her shoulder. She had already turned and began walking down the hallway in the opposite direction.

"Excuse me." A tall, burly man came barreling past me in a Willow Glen Fire Station t-shirt, matching pants, and steeled toed boots. He gripped a box of ornaments tightly with a look of determination on his face. I sidestepped him and then entered the room as he called out over his shoulder. "Brown, where do you want these?"

I followed his gaze and resisted the urge to smile. Monae stood in the corner near the front of the dining hall speaking with one of the residents that had wandered in. Without breaking gaze from the person she was speaking to, she pointed to the opposite side of the room where boxes were stacked next to an impressive amount of craft store bags. The tall man nodded and placed the box down.

"Hey," he said, turning to face me. "You work here?"

"No. I'm catering the food. I'm with The Hungry Hippo." I offered the guy a handshake. He snorted after hearing the name of the restaurant and shook my hand quickly; his skin was clammy and damp. I had to fight the urge to wipe my hand on my pants. "Do you need any help with those?"

"Yeah sure, that'd be great. Brown went overboard on the decorations." He rolled his eyes affectionately. From the small smile on his lips, I could tell he cared deeply about Monae, or 'Brown' as he called her. He reached down to grab another box near the door. "I'm Sean, by the way."

"Jai." Monae hadn't noticed me yet and I used it as an opportunity to watch her as she spoke with the elderly lady. Her hair was in braids that had been put in a large bun at the back of her head. She wore the same uniform as Sean and the other guys that were bringing in the supplies, but somehow, it looked different on her.

"Nice to meet you, Jai." I looked back at Sean to find him grinning at me. He had seen me shamelessly staring at Monae. "She's a force."

"Who do you mean?" I tried my best to feign ignorance, but Sean's grin widened, telling me he didn't buy it for a second.

"Monae. She's like a sister to me, but I'm not blind to the effect she has on people." He handed me a box.

"Guilty as charged, I guess." I laughed. "Am I that obvious?"

"You might as well hold a sign that says 'Monae please notice me' in big red letters. It's all over your face."

I resisted the urge to smile. It seemed like everyone but Monae noticed how far gone I was over her. I glanced over at her to see that she had concluded her conversation with the resident and was wiping the tables and sighed quietly. Before I could stop myself, I felt my feet carrying me in her direction.

"Hey."

She glanced up at me and smiled politely, "Hey, Jai. You here to help decorate the trees?"

"What kind of money do elves use?" I blurted, before I had a chance to stop myself. Her eyes narrowed as she studied me. I waited, feeling the embarrassment creep further up my spine the longer it took her to respond.

"What kind?"

"Jingle bills." I replied with a sheepish shrug.

To my surprise, she snorted. "God, that's a terrible joke."

She was right. It was terrible but it was the first thing that came to mind while I was scrambling for something to say. Out of the corner of my eye, I saw Sean shake his head as he continued to stack boxes. Not my best work, but at least it caught her attention. With a smile, I motioned towards what she was working on.

"Do you need any help?"

"Sure. We are setting up for the residents to be able to design their own ornaments to put on the trees. I'm working on organizing the supplies so everything will be easy to grab." She handed me a stack of glittery pens, "Can you put a few of these on each table for me?"

"Ay Ay Captain!" I grabbed the pens and turned away before the look on her face could make the embarrassment settle in any further. It wasn't usually this hard talking to someone I was attracted to, but Monae made my mouth get dry and my hands start to sweat.

"So what are you even doing here today?" Monae's voice chimed in behind me as I placed the pens on each table. "I looked at the menu and we're getting sandwiches from the shop down the street."

My back stiffened, I hadn't expected to be caught so soon. I continued placing the pens while I scrambled for an excuse. "Um..."

"Excuse me! Is this where the decorating is going to be?" a thin voice interrupted before I could stick my foot any further in my mouth. A quiet sigh of relief escaped my lips as we both turned to see who had spoken.

An elderly woman with warm brown skin, high cheekbones, and kind eyes looked back at us. The silvery gray hair that framed her face almost sparkled under the light. The yellow cardigan she wore was draped over her thin shoulders. She studied the both of us with a sharp gaze, the hint of a smile on her lips. She radiated warmth and tenderness with fine lines in her face that hinted of years full of grace and wisdom. She hadn't said more than a few words, but something about her presence was comforting. I believe Monae felt it too, because her face broke into a genuine smile. Her own warmth and radiance swirling around the three of us.

"Absolutely! We are still setting up, but you are welcome to take a seat at one of these tables while we-"

She threw up a hand, causing Monae to stop abruptly, "Nonsense. I may be old, but I can still move around just fine. Put me to work."

"Yes Ma'am. Follow me. I'm Monae. It's nice to meet you Ms.-?"

"Birdie Mae." She replied with a quick nod.

I watched as the two of them headed back to the section where Monae had stacked all of the items that needed to be put on the tables. Something told me that this wouldn't be the last we'd see of Birdie Mae.

Just as we were finishing the last few moments of set up, a staff member poked her head into the room with a cheerful smile on her face. "Are you guys ready to get started? I have a group of residents out here waiting that are super excited to come in! Can we- hey! Birdie, how'd you get in here?"

The elderly woman turned and smirked at the staff member. "I walked in on these two old legs, Jennifer. At my age, who gon' stop me?"

Jennifer sighed and shook her head, "Alright everybody! You can come in and take a seat so we can get started!"

Monae, Sean, and three other firefighters I hadn't had the chance to speak to, headed to the front of the room. It was mesmerizing watching how she moved through the room with confidence. She had never seemed insecure, but there was a different aura about her in uniform.

"Hello, everyone. My name is Monae Brown. This is Sean Pittman, Anthony Branch, Percy Arnold, Ashton Daniels, and Thurman Normil." She pointed to each man as she called out their names. Each of them gave a small wave or a nod when they were mentioned. Seeing the way they deferred to her for leadership was admirable, if not a little intimidating.

"The plan is to make some ornaments for the Christmas trees and then bake cookies, but I was told that cookies absolutely had to come first." She threw a quick grin in Birdie's direction, who nodded in approval. "So, if everyone can wash their hands, we will begin the cookie baking experience!"

As the small group of residents filed into the kitchen to begin washing their hands so they could begin cookie decorating, Monae gave me a sidelong look. "Guess we're about to see if your baking skills are better than your comedy."

My grin was immediate. "Can't be worse."

Something swelled inside of me as she rolled her eyes and bumped my shoulder with hers. The gesture was small, but it was enough to make my heart thud a little harder. I'd been pining away for this girl for a few years now, secretly plotting to make my move. Maybe, just maybe, I was closer than I thought.

Chapter Three

Monae

The smell of burning chocolate wafted through the entire kitchen. I had stepped out for just a few minutes to take a phone call and chaos had erupted as soon as I'd left. Billows of smoke wafted from all three ovens. The residents sat glued to their chairs, fear and concern on their faces while Jai frantically hurried around the kitchen waving a dish towel in front of the smoke detector that was currently beeping angrily.

I glanced around the room in search of my currently useless coworkers. All four of them had wandered off somewhere, not paying any attention to any of the residents and what they were doing. Even Branch, who was usually vigilant about cooking safety, was nowhere to be found.

"Monae! Honey, please help him." Birdie called from her seat next to an elderly gentleman. She flicked a hand over her shoulder at Jai, who was beginning to break a sweat with his choppy and frantic movements. "He's going to send us to the grave too early!"

I snorted at her comment as I located the fire extinguisher. Watching Jai flail about in an unproductive panic made me shake my head. As the co-owner of a popular restaurant, you'd think basic fire safety was lodged in his brain by now. As many times as my team and I have taken turns doing inspections over there, it was disappointing to see that nothing we'd taught him stuck.

The smoke clung to the air, sharp and sugary, as I snatched the extinguisher from its spot on the wall and quickly put out the fires. I had just shoved it back into its spot when Pittman and Branch reentered the room, surveying the scene in surprise.

"The hell happened here?" Pittman asked, turning to me. I ignored him for the moment and directed my attention to Jai, who stood holding the charred tray like some sort of literal burnt offering.

"Seriously? I step out of the room for two minutes and you managed to completely ruin six dozen cookies. You own a restaurant! Shouldn't this be second nature?"

Jai grinned widely at me, his expression sheepish. "I run the numbers. Not the oven. Thankfully."

Before I could answer, a laugh cackled from across the room. Birdie wagged a finger at Jai like this was the most entertainment she'd seen in a long time.

"This one here couldn't boil water without setting off an alarm. Handsome face, useless hands."

Jai's grin widened, "All I heard was that you think I'm handsome."

"Hmph. Useless ears too." she shot back, an amused smile curling the corners of her mouth.

brushes in her hand. She looked down. The woman's blood was smeared down one arm of her denim jacket, where she'd reached in to undo the seat belt. Yuck. And where was the passing traffic? No cars out tonight? Not *one* car taking this shortcut through the back of Ponsonby on a Tuesday night after midnight? That figured. She knocked on the door harder. Finally, it opened.

An old geezer stood in his mental-ward-blue pajamas and paisley bathrobe, tied tight. He kept the door's safety chain on, a flimsy, piece of gold chain like a necklace promising lifelong love. He squinted through the gap. "What do you want?"

"This woman's had an accident. See?" Because he really ought to have figured that out already, unless he was completely deaf, "Can you call an ambulance? Please?"

"What's the number?" he asked, gruff and short.

Bless him. A geriatric with attitude. It would've been quicker to saunter down to the losers on the front porch couch and smoke a big doobie and let the woman walk herself home.

"God, I don't know! I think it's... 911! No, it's not 911. It's..." She had no idea. She'd never had to call an ambulance. All those stupid American TV shows were to blame. They'd gone and gotten imbedded in her brain—the American number for ambulances was all she could think of. "Call 0. Call the operator on 0 and ask them."

The old man squinted at her, his forehead wrinkled up like a dachshund's skin, like his heckles rising at the full moon, recoiling from the fully blown signs of insanity he figured he was facing down on his doorstep.

"Are you drunk, miss?"

"What? No. Listen. Just call the operator. Dial 0. Get an ambulance. This Woman Cannot Be Moved!'"

Without another word, the old geezer shut the door. Moments later his light switched off.

She could hear the car hissing away behind her. It wasn't like she was hallucinating, or making this shit up, the car crash was right there in plain view. Bastard. Where was his *humanity*? She turned, jumped up with adrenaline, grabbed a handful of ragged gravel from the guy's path and lobed it at his bay window. Nothing broke. More's the pity. She returned to the woman, who had half of her handbag spilled into her lap and was ferreting through her things, trying to find key evidence to destroy before she was carted away by the authorities, perhaps. She saw a phone among the detritus.

"Hey, you've got a phone! Okay. *We're* gonna call the ambulance."

The woman's fingers curled around the phone. She started sobbing, "No. I don't want to make any calls."

"What? Please. Just pass me the phone. I'll take care of it."

The woman snatched it away, hiding it down by the handbrake. She'd actually pulled the handbrake. It was up as far as it could go. The automatic transmission was still in 'D,' though. The phone was far from reach, with the woman bent over to protect it. The bare side of her stomach protruded from between her top and black trousers. She started dialing with her red nails that weren't even chipped. The blood still trickled from her chin and forehead. She held the phone up to her ear. To the good side of her head. The other side still bled and her hair was matted into another wound on the back of

"Mm." He replied, his gaze too steady. "Funny thing is, it didn't feel like you were watching me for smoke alarms."

I swallowed, unsure of what to say to deflect. How do you tell someone you don't know that well that you were thinking about what it was like to be with them? Wouldn't that be weird?

"Don't flatter yourself." I scoffed, my voice sounding as unsure as I felt.

"Must have imagined it, then" he said softly, amusement flickering behind his expression.

I stayed silent as he turned and headed out into the room where the residents were setting up to begin making the Christmas decorations, taking the warmth that was creeping up my shoulders with him.

"Alright, tell me everything you know about Jai Carter." I hissed into the phone. It was two days later, and I'd finally gotten the chance to call Audrey.

"Hello to you too. Why yes, I'm doing well, Mon, thanks for asking, how are you?" she replied sarcastically. I rolled my eyes and flopped backwards on the bed. Blaze huffed softly as my head smacked into his side. I shifted to give him extra room on the bed.

"Now is not the time for jokes, woman. I need answers."

"What do you want to know?"

"Tell me something. Anything."

"I mean he's a pretty cool guy he- wait...why?"

I stayed silent, staring up at the ceiling while I waited for her to connect the dots. It didn't take long. There was a second of silence before an ear-piercing squeal split the air.

"THE JOURNAL IS SETTING YOU UP WITH JAI?!"

I flinched, "I don't know if I'd say all that just yet."

"Monae!"

"Okay, fine. The journal mentioned something about my match not being who I expected. Sometimes it doesn't arrive in a blaze, sometimes it's burnt cookies. blah blah." I waved my hand in the air, trying to dismiss the nerves that were bubbling up in my stomach.

"And?" She pressed.

"And Jai burned the crap out of the cookies we were making for the residents. I'm talking flames, smoke, alarms, the whole nine. The place still smells like a bonfire."

The sound of her laughter brought a smile to my face. "That tracks. He's a businessman through and through, but Montrell handles all of the cooking."

"What can you tell me about him?"

"He's a great guy. He takes risks and as a result, both The Hungry Hippo and Audrey's Kitchen have both been thriving."

"What else?" I reached over and scratched Blaze behind the ears.

"He doesn't know his own charm, but he is one of the most loyal and kindhearted guys you could meet. When he wants something, he goes for it, no matter the risk."

"Okay I-"

"Oh! And he tells terrible jokes when he's nervous. It's his tell."

I froze at her last comment, my mind going back to when he approached me at the nursing home. He didn't seem nervous at the time, but he did blurt out a joke when I acknowledged him. I thought on it for a moment. Could he have been nervous? That didn't make much sense to me because we had spoken a few times before. We had seen each other at the cooking contest a few years back and then off and on since then. Why would he be nervous now? "Monae? You still there?"

I shifted, realizing that I had let the line go quiet while I replayed the events of the other day in my head. "Yeah, I'm here, just thinking."

"For what it's worth, friend, I think you and Jai would be cute together. He's so laid back and you're so-"

"So what?" I pressed after she paused.

"You can be a little...serious sometimes." she said gently, like she was trying to avoid hurting my feelings. "I think he could help you lighten up some."

"Am I that bad?" I laughed.

"No, I never said 'bad'. Make no mistake, you're an amazing woman, but I think with your job, you tend to carry the weight of the world on your shoulders. It'd be nice to see you let someone else carry the load a little."

Her words settled deep into my chest. There was a lot of downtime where I chose to work, but that didn't shake the fact that I had seen some really ugly calls in my time at the station. I thought I did a pretty good job of leaving it at work, but sometimes I couldn't help bringing it home with me. Families ripped apart by devastating fires and accidents that could have been prevented. It was hard not to carry it around on my shoulders sometimes.

A quiet rustling caught my attention. Blaze and I both looked over at my desk where the journal and its pen had been. Now, the pages were flipping back and forth in a dramatic show. Instead of the normal excitement that my girls had said they felt when the journal was crafting a new entry, a sense of dread washed over me. If Jai was supposed to be my match, what did that mean for me? It had been a while since I'd paid any attention to my dating life. If my job didn't intimidate them, my stoic demeanor usually did. If I let my heart open to the possibility of Jai, what if he also couldn't handle it? What if he didn't even like me to begin with and I was letting this journal put ideas in my head that didn't need to be there?

"I'll call you back, love. I have to prep for the next shift." I vaguely registered Audrey ending the conversation. I let the phone slide out of my hand as soon as I heard the click on her end, my attention completely on the journal.

"What do I do, Blazey Boy?" I whispered. He stared at me like I'd lost my mind and turned back to his nap, leaving me to face the journal by myself. With a sigh, I slid off the bed and stepped over to my desk.

DEAR DIARY,

DISASTER DOESN'T ALWAYS MEAN DESTRUCTION. AT TIMES, IT SPARKS THE CONNECTION TWO HEARTS HAVE BEEN WAITING FOR, BUT ONLY IF THEY ARE BOTH BRAVE ENOUGH TO STEP TOWARD IT. SHE SAVED THE DAY, LIKE SHE ALWAYS DOES, BUT PERHAPS SHE OVERLOOKED THE LESSON HIDDEN IN THE SMOKE.

THE ONE SHE LEAST EXPECTED MAY BE THE ONE THAT HOLDS THE ANSWER HER HEART HAD BEEN QUIETLY SEARCHING FOR ALL ALONG, BUT ANSWERS ARE

Chapter Four

Jai

I leaned against the prep table in the back of The Hungry Hippo, giving Montrell a quick rundown of everything that happened, and didn't happen, with the cookies. He listened as he rinsed out a mixing bowl and hummed quietly like nothing in the world could rattle him. After being with Audrey and being in different situations that required quick thinking, chaos in the kitchen had become his happy place. Me, not so much.

He finally stopped humming and shot me an amused look. "So let me make sure I'm hearing you correctly. You, co-owner of a successful restaurant, burned two dozen cookies. At a nursing home Christmas event?"

"Don't say it like that." I winced.

"How else should I say it?" He tossed the dishrag in the sink with a soft thud and turned to wash his hands. "I shouldn't phrase it like you almost smoked out a room full of eighty-year-olds? Man, they're already on Heaven's doorstep and you over here trying to push them through!"

I sighed. "You're a terrible person. Truly. Ten out of ten do not recommend."

He barked out a laugh as he reached for the tomatoes and the cutting board next to the sink. "I'm calling it like I see it. So, what did Monae do? Let me guess, she swooped in with her fireman's cape and saved the day?"

"Something like that." I mumbled, glancing away.

"My herooo!" Montrell swooned, batting his eyes like a lovestruck girl in a romance movie. I tossed a napkin at his head and laughed.

"What do you want me to say, 'Trell? She makes me nervous."

He scoffed. "Nervous? I've seen you negotiate with suppliers until they're blue in the face and charm your way into unheard of opportunities, but one woman walks in the room and suddenly you forget how an oven works?"

"She's not just any woman. She's-She's Monae." I shot back. "She looked good. Like crazy good."

"If you're burning ready-made cookie dough, you're too far gone already. Might as well tattoo her name across your forehead. Add a little heart next to it so she knows it's real."

I laughed, even though part of me hated how accurate he was. Whenever I'm around her, Monae doesn't just get in my head. She seeps her way into everything. My hands, my rhythm, my confidence, and my every move. No matter how hard I tried to calm my nerves whenever we were in the same room, my heart thudded in my chest at a scary pace.

"Okay, I've packed everything you'll need for the meal today and I've written explicit instructions." Montrell said as he placed the last tray of food in my truck. "I'd say that it'd be impossible for you to screw it up, but we saw how you performed with cookies."

"Are you ever going to let this go?" I asked, narrowing my eyes. He had been finding ways to tease me all morning.

"It'll be the last thing I say on my deathbed."

"Hopefully that's sooner rather than later."

He laughed and then smacked me on the shoulder. "Don't get mad because I can bake a dessert without turning the building into a fire hazard."

I was due to be at the nursing home in twenty minutes. Today was their ugly sweater event. The Hungry Hippo had agreed to provide the lunch: Baked Feta Soup, Tuscan Chicken Wraps, and Butternut Squash Potstickers for the few vegan residents. Audrey had made mini–Christmas Trifles for dessert. Montrell had taped instructions to the tops of the oven ready pans and texted them to me one by one. I knew he was being funny, but I was grateful for the extra instructions. Hopefully, I wouldn't make too much of a mess of things. It wouldn't be good for business if I kept burning the food to a crisp before anyone could taste it.

By the time I made it to the nursing home, the combinations of food smells in my truck were making my stomach rumble. My nerves had been too jumbled to think about eating. I wanted to make sure I got everything into the kitchen and in the ovens without issue. The last thing I needed was to accidentally spill something or trip over my own feet while I was bringing in the dishes.

Sean was leaving the building as I entered carrying two trays. He held the door open for me with a huge smile. "Hey, man! That smells amazing already. Need any help?"

"Actually, yes. My truck is right there." I tilted my head in the direction of my truck. "I have a few more trays. Mind bringing them in?"

"Got it." He raced off as I headed towards the kitchen, praying there would be staff in there that could keep an eye on things so nothing went wrong.

The nursing home looked a little less depressing as I walked through the halls and toward the kitchen. Residents had decorated their doors and hung Christmas lights down the corridor walls. Soft Christmas music played from somewhere and the nurses I passed had on Santa hats and reindeer ears. It was a little less doom and gloom and made me feel underdressed. I hadn't bothered to find an ugly Christmas sweater. I'd assumed I would be hiding in the kitchen stalking the food as it warmed to make sure it didn't burn. As much as I wanted to participate, my main mission was the food. I could steal a glance at Monae later on.

"Good morning, honey. I was hoping you'd come back today." Birdie Mae's voice cut through my thoughts. I turned, a smile already on my face.

"Ms. Birdie! Of course, I wouldn't miss another chance to see you."

She smirked and then glanced at the food trays, "Do you have someone to help you with this? It seems like a great deal of work for one person."

"You offering?" I asked. Sean stepped around Birdie's small frame to set the last few trays on the counter. I nodded in his direction as a thank you.

Her eyes lit up. "It's been a long time since I've been able to get in the kitchen. Put me to work."

Birdie moved with surprising ease and agility in the kitchen. Although there wasn't much to do but prep the ovens and then plate the food after everything had warmed, she seemed excited to be able to be in this environment.

"Cooking used to be how I relaxed." She offered, as if she could read my thoughts. I nodded and took the pan out of her hands to place it in the preheated oven. "You don't seem as...frazzled as you did with the cookies."

"I'm not usually that much of a disaster in the kitchen."

"So, what happened?"

Before I could respond, it felt like the air in the room shifted. I glanced up to see Monae standing in the doorway. She was wearing the same Willow Glen Fire Station T-shirt and pants that I saw her in the other day, but it still caused me to stop in my tracks. Birdie Mae followed my gaze, a flicker of understanding softened her expression.

"Hey, Ms. Birdie. It's almost time for the ugly sweater competition. Are you ready?" Monae made a show of looking at her outfit. The rich green sweater and brown capris hinted at a good deal of money and fashion sense, but not an ugly sweater contest.

"Oh! I almost forgot about that. I have my sweater back in my room. Jai," She turned to me with a tight smile, "Help me, please?"

I tilted my head, confused. "You need my help getting a sweater?"

Her answer was sharp and left no room for arguing. "Yes. Now, come."

I put down what I was holding, casting a sidelong glance at the oven. I didn't want to travel too far for fear of repeating yesterday's damage but I could tell that Birdie was not the type of woman you fought against. If she asked you to do something, she expected it to be done. Grown man or not, I didn't want to run the risk of getting in trouble. With a sigh, I turned on my heel and followed after Birdie who had already made it a good distance down the hallway.

"Try to keep up." She called over her shoulder.

When we got to her room, she gestured for me to come in. I hesitated in the doorway, feeling unsure and not wanting to intrude. Sensing my hesitation, she turned to me and made a face. "If I didn't want you to come in, I wouldn't have brought you down here. Come in and close my door. I don't need that nosey Bernadette two doors down all in my business."

I stepped inside, suddenly feeling like I was being transported into a different world. The bland, gloomy decor did not cross over into Birdie Mae's room. The walls were a deep shade of navy with expertly placed gold accents to naturally bring your gaze across the room. The room smelled faintly of expensive perfume.

"So, how long have you liked that girl?" Her question was abrupt, like a record scratch.

I blinked, "Excuse me?"

"Monae." She said it like it was the most obvious thing in the world. "I might be old, but I'm not blind."

We stood silently, looking at each other in a stand off. Seeing who would break first. I did. I sighed and shook my head. "Am I that obvious?"

"Maybe not. But you stare at her the same way my Simon used to stare at me. Like she's your favorite movie and you're scared someone will turn off the television if you look away."

Her words struck something deep in my chest. "Simon was your husband, right?"

It was her turn to sigh. A soft, wistful smile spread across her face, softening her expression. "He was a tall drink of hot chocolate on a cold winter day. And hopelessly in love with me from the moment we met. Followed me around like a love-sick puppy for a full year before I finally gave in and let him take me to a drive in. Best decision I ever made."

"You didn't like him at first?" I asked, stepping towards some of the golden framed photos on her walls.

"Oh no," she laughed, "I was just as smitten with him, but I wanted to see that he was truly interested first."

Pictures of Birdie Mae and a tall man, I assume was Simon, in various ages and stages of life were all over her walls. In a few of the pictures, another lady stood with them. I turned to Birdie.

"Who is this?"

She stepped closer and squinted at the picture. "Oh! That is my best friend, Amada Williams. She is the reason my Simon and I got together. Well, her journal was."

I wanted to push further, but she waved a hand and ducked into her closet. The moment had passed. When she stepped out, she had an older sweater in her hands. It was red with a crooked reindeer in the middle. "Here. This was his. He wore it every Christmas, even after I told him it was the ugliest sweater I had ever seen. He'd put it on and do a silly little dance that would make me laugh every single time."

I took the sweater carefully, like it would disintegrate in my hands if I wasn't gentle. "Are you sure? This feels too sentimental for me to wear."

She nodded. "I am. Simon would have loved you and if we want to make an impression on Monae, then we need to pull out the big guns. I don't think burning the cookies was the right way to do it."

That made me laugh. The sound broke through the tension that was settling on my shoulders and in my chest. "Thank you, Ms. Birdie. This really means a lot."

"Don't thank me yet." She waved a hand towards the bathroom door. "It still has to work first. Go put it on and show that girl you've got some charm under there. Please don't burn the meal today. My appetite is cooperating for once and I do not want that slop they usually pass as food around here."

When I stepped back into the main room, wearing Simon's old sweater, Monae was pulling the chairs around to resemble a catwalk. She had changed out of her t-shirt into a dark green sweater with jumbled Christmas lights on the front and a battery pack crudely glued under her arm.

"I like your sweater." I said, as I approached her. She turned to look at me, taking in the crooked reindeer and grinned.

"Wow. This is...festive."

I struck a silly pose, making her laugh even harder. The sound spread warmth through my chest. "Birdie Mae insisted. She said it was her husband Simon's sweater, and I didn't want to disappoint her. Tis the season and all."

"That's really sweet." Monae said softly.

A silence settled over the both of us. I studied her and she held my gaze in a way that felt like we were the only two in the room. My body was itching to move closer to her, to take in the faint scent of vanilla that filled the air whenever she moved, but instead, I cleared my throat awkwardly and smiled.

"Do you think I'll win the contest?"

She rolled her eyes, smiling wide, "Not a chance. I do think you could win 'Most Likely to Blind you with Christmas Cheer' though."

"Is that a category?"

"No, but we can make a special exception for you."

"I think your sweater would be a better fit for that. You're covered in lights."

She hit the battery pack under her arm so the lights would begin to flash all over her sweater. She winked at me and then went back to sorting the chairs as the residents began shuffling in the room. I used that as my cue to go check on the food. Some of the kitchen staff had been in there to keep an eye on things. As I headed into the kitchen, I couldn't help but smile down at the good luck charm Birdie Mae had given me.

This sweater looked like it had seen one too many Christmases, but if it brought me any closer to being with Monae, I'd wear it as long as I had to.

Chapter Five
Monae

"So, Audrey told us that the journal was pointing you towards Jai." Elodie grabbed a slice of pizza and took a bite. "I've been dying to know what's been happening."

The five of us were huddled into my apartment, having our usual book club meeting. We had decided to start the Delgato Family books by Jahquel J. The first one was Capone and as much as I had heard people hyping up this world she had created, I was excited to get into it.

"Not much has really happened yet." I replied, shrugging. "He burned the fool out of some cookies though. The kitchen still smelled like smoke when we came back for the ugly sweater contest."

Audrey winced. "Trell said that he was really embarrassed about that. How did the food turn out on day two though?"

"It was amazing. Those potstickers were delicious. And that trifle?" I clutched a hand to my chest. "Sent from Heaven."

Brina expertly flopped down next to me on the couch, managing to not spill her drink or her plate of food. "You seem apprehensive about the whole thing, Mon."

"I am!" I wailed. "Jai is a sweet guy, he just seems so...goofy."

"He can be, but I've been told that he has a serious side as well."

"I haven't seen it." I took a bite of my pizza. "The journal keeps telling me to let go of my expectations and open myself up to something new, blah blah."

"You could definitely stand to be a little less uptight, friend." Deja said slowly. She had been scrolling on her phone and acting like she wasn't listening, but I knew she'd chime in eventually. "You're so serious sometimes."

"I've been told." I rolled my eyes and took a sip of my wine. "He seems like such a lighthearted type. What makes you think he'd even be able to handle me?"

Audrey flashed me a knowing smile, "I guess you'll just have to find out."

I had just entered the station when my phone buzzed in my pocket. I pulled it out and glanced down at it. Whispering Pines flashed across the screen.

"Hello?" I answered, as I put my things in my locker. Tomorrow was supposed to be the Christmas treat event. Cookies were at the top of the list, since Jai had wanted to redeem himself from a few days before. We had a list of other treats to make as well.

"Monae?" Mrs. Raeford, the director of nursing, sounded frantic. I immediately perked up.

"Hi. What's wrong?"

"We've got an emergency. Can you stop by?" My mind raced with the possibilities. Was someone hurt? Did someone get sick? Why didn't she call for emergency services if something was going on? I grabbed my keys and my jacket and headed to my car.

"I'm on my way."

By the time I'd made it to the nursing home, the tension had built up in my shoulders. I could feel it all over. Mrs. Raeford sat in her office on the phone. She held up a finger when I entered.

"Can you have someone come take a look at it soon at least?" I waited as she paused, listening to the other person on the line. "Thank God. Okay, when you arrive, have someone ask for me, please. I'll show you where the problem is. Thank you."

"Is everything okay?" I blurted, as soon as she hung up.

"The freezer is out." She sighed, her entire body sagged back in her chair. "Everything we prepped for tomorrow is spoiled. The butter, the cookie dough, the eggs, the milk. It's all inedible. If we can't replace it by today, the treat event will have to be canceled."

My heart sank. The residents had been excited for this moment; I'd heard whispers about it from those who hadn't participated in any of the other events. News had traveled quickly that we were going to have Christmas treats and a quick concert full of Christmas carols, everybody had wanted to come.

"Okay." I sorted through the possible options in my head. "We can absolutely come up with a solution. Maybe we can-"

My voice cut short as I glanced behind me and made eye contact with Jai. I hadn't expected him to be standing there. I assumed, in her panic, Mrs. Raeford had called him as well. She ushered him into the office, completely oblivious to the way my voice had trailed off at the sight of him.

"What's wrong?" he asked, glancing at my expression.

"The freezers are out. Everything we've prepped for the baking portion of the Christmas events is completely spoiled." I managed to choke out.

"The residents were really looking forward to that." he replied simply, turning to Mrs. Raeford, "What are our options?"

"I've got my guy coming in to look at the freezers in about an hour. He'll be able to determine what the issue was, but we exceeded the budget just trying to get the first batch of items."

"We can take a look in the pantry and see what is available." I offered. "It may not be as much, but it'll be fine."

"I'll handle it."

I turned to look at Jai, startled at the tone of his voice. He was already pulling his phone out. The set of his shoulders and the clipped way he replied, made me pause.

"Handle it how?" I demanded, crossing my arms, "I've got this, Jai. This is more serious than a quick store run. We need-"

"Trust me." he said, meeting my gaze. His voice was calm but there was a firmness there that I wasn't used to. He left no room for protest.

"Marcus." He said gruffly into the phone, "You got a second?"

I heard a low response as he stepped to the side to take the call. I watched in awe as his jaw flexed, and his entire posture shifted to match the seriousness in his tone. He remained steady, even as the man on the other end pushed back on what he was asking. Jai's voice dropped lower, smooth but commanding and I couldn't tear my eyes away.

"Ooh, look at him go." Birdie Mae's voice momentarily pulled me out of my trance. I blinked, turning to her. I hadn't heard her walk up, but there she stood in the doorway, a knowing smile on her face. "You seeing this?"

I said nothing, because yes. I absolutely was seeing it. And feeling it. Normally, I was the one to step in and take charge of a situation. Seeing someone else take the reins so effortlessly was...different. By the time Jai had hung up, my pulse was ticking a little bit faster than it was before. I could feel the heat rising on my neck and into my cheeks.

"You'll have a delivery by six tonight," he said simply.

Mrs. Raeford's shoulders slumped once again, "Oh, thank God. You've saved the day, Mr. Carter."

"That ain't all he did." Birdie Mae grinned at me like she could read every single thought swimming around in my head. If I wasn't worried it would hurt her, I'd stomp on her foot in this moment to get her to hush. But there was no hushing this woman.

I cleared my throat, awkwardly trying and failing to tamp down the warmth that was spreading through my entire body. "That was...impressive."

That crooked grin I was starting to enjoy, slid across his face confidently. "It's what I do. In the meantime-" he turned to Mrs. Raeford, "show me the freezers. I could probably fix the issue, depending on what it is."

"Sure. Come with me." She stood from her desk and grabbed her keys. As we all stepped out of her office, now that the crisis had been fully averted.

"I can come back around six and wait for the truck." I offered, feeling useless in the moment.

Jai turned to me, for a beat the air between us felt charged. "You don't have to. I can wait. Ms. Birdie owes me a rematch on a Gin Rummy game anyway. Pretty sure she cheated."

"Don't confuse your lack of skill with me being dishonest, young man." Birdie Mae's eyes narrowed at Jai, but there was a playfulness in her tone. He chuckled as he turned and followed Mrs. Raeford to the kitchen, oblivious to the way my heart was thudding wildly in my chest.

Goofy is what I had called him, not serious enough. I'd written him off as the boy next door with the crooked grin and the bad jokes, but standing here watching him effortlessly take control of the situation had me recoloring the picture I had painted of him.

I couldn't get the image of Jai out of my head. The way he'd handled the vendor earlier, calm but firm without even raising his voice, it had done something weird in my chest. It wasn't just that he'd saved the day. It was how he did it. So effortless and confident.

Steady. Like he had been just looking for a moment to jump in and show what he was capable of. The moment had been playing on a never-ending loop in my head. Even after I went back to the station and completed a good portion of my shift. As I drove back to Whispering Pines and now as I sat in the recreation room, unsure of what to do. The journal had been oddly silent, I admit that I peeked at it, hoping for some guidance but it remained empty aside from the last few entries I'd already read.

"You've got that look on your face." I glanced to my left to see Birdie Mae leaning against the doorway, arms folded as if she was ready to scold me.

"What look?"

"The one I'd always get on my face when I was about to yell at my Simon or kiss him. And if I had to guess, today is not the yelling type of day."

I blanched, almost choking on my water. "Excuse me?"

Her grin widened. She shuffled closer and gingerly sat down in the seat across from me. "Don't play innocent with me, girl. I've seen it brewing between the two of you from the first day. You don't think I notice how you two are always watching each other? Every time you're not looking at him, he's looking at you and vice versa."

"That's not true, I-"

"You were ready and willing to take over, but as soon as Jai stepped in and handled the situation, you got all gooey eyed. It's cute."

I groaned. "I did not get all gooey-eyed. You make me sound like the lovesick damsel in distress."

"What's wrong with that?" She grinned.

"I am not a damsel in distress. I am fully capable of handling myself and taking care of myself." I shot back, rolling my eyes.

"As black women, we are conditioned to believe that we need to carry the load at all times. If we aren't shouldering the burden then we consider ourselves weak." She reached out and patted my hand, "But there is nothing wrong with letting a man step in. Especially one like him."

"One like him?" I repeated.

"Oh, yes." Her grin widened. "He's got that good mix. Deny it all you like, but a man like him doesn't come around often. Goofy enough to make you laugh, but solid enough to make you feel safe."

My face felt hot. "You're imagining things."

"Maybe. Or maybe you're just scared." She patted my hand again, a little firmer this time, "You are scared to admit that you like this easy-going man that makes you smile. Scared to admit that something about him intrigues you."

I had no comeback for that one.

She smirked, realizing she had me cornered. "I tell you what, he told me that he loves hot chocolate with a little splash of peppermint. Go to that Flashbucks place you kids like and get him some."

"Starbucks?" I chuckled.

"You knew what I meant." She shrugged, pulling herself up from her seat. "Stop being afraid and go take him a drink as a thank you for saving the treats."

I sat there, gaping after her in shock. But, an hour later, there I stood, outside of The Hungry Hippo, gripping two red cups full of hot chocolate like an idiot. My heart hammered in my chest.

There was a lull before the dinner rush began. I glanced at the clock on the wall. He would most likely be heading back to Whispering Pines to wait for the truck soon. I'd wanted to catch him before he left. I stood by the door, unsure of what to do or how to announce my presence. He stood at the cash register with his back to me, a pile of receipts stacked next to him.

"You going to keep standing there staring," he called without looking up, "Or are you going to say something?"

"I wasn't staring." I blurted, heat making my cheeks flush.

"Right. My mistake." He finally turned to look at me, grinning. "Is that for me?"

"Yes. It's hot chocolate." I crossed the room and placed the cup in front of him. "Don't get used to it. It's just a thank you for helping out earlier."

His grin deepened and I felt every bit of it in my stomach. "So, you were impressed?"

I tried to scoff, but it came out more like a nervous laugh. "I'm impressed that you didn't screw it up. If that's what you mean. You were very...um...."

He chuckled as my voice faltered. He studied me for a moment and then leaned forward across the counter, bringing our faces closer together. But not too close. Not yet.

"You know," his voice was low and soft, "You don't have to do everything yourself. It's okay to lean on...someone every now and then."

"Are you referring to yourself?" I asked.

"Only if you want me to be." he replied, looking down at my lips and letting his gaze take its time reaching my eyes. When they did, the heat behind them caught me off guard. My body responded in a way I didn't expect as his words landed somewhere deep.

"I think," I began, voice shaking imperceptibly, "I think I do."

Chapter Six
Monae

DEAR DiARY,

CHOCOLATE CAN BE MORE THAN JUST A SWEET TREAT, iT CAN BE A PEACE OFFERiNG. A BRiDGE OR A DOOR. TODAY, SHE OPENED THAT DOOR, EVEN iF iT WAS ONLY A CRACK. THE MAN WHO MAKES HER LAUGH ALSO MADE HER HEART SKiTTER iN HER CHEST, THOUGH SHE'LL DENY iT iF ASKED.

SOME SPARKS COME FROM ?RE, OTHERS COME FROM QUiET MOMENTS SHARED ACROSS A COUNTERTOP. HE'S MORE THAN JOKES AND AN EASY-GOiNG NATURE. THERE'S STEEL UNDER THAT GRiN, AND iT MiGHT BE EXACTLY WHAT SHE NEEDS. iF SHE LETS HERSELF TAKE THAT CHANCE.

I re-read the entry with one eye open. It had been waiting for me last night after I came home from dropping off the hot chocolate for Jai. He'd made his interest in me quite clear, but something in me was still too nervous to make a solid move. I had confirmed that I wanted him to be the one I could lean on, but after that, I clammed up. The conversation got awkward, and I couldn't remember what I had really wanted to say.

I took a screenshot of the diary entry, sent it to the group chat and then rolled out of the bed to start my day. Not even two minutes later and my phone started buzzing angrily. There was only one person that would be calling my phone this early.

"You better have a good reason for calling me before the clock even reaches double digits." I grumbled into the phone as I shuffled my feet into the kitchen to make a cup of coffee. Blaze trudged behind me, bumping into the back of my leg when I stopped to grab my charger.

Deja's laugh was far too awake for this hour. "Girl, hush. You know you were already awake. You Firefighter types are basically just roosters with nicer biceps."

"What do you want?" I rolled my eyes, even though she couldn't see me.

"Just wanted to hear what you had to say after that little screenshot you tried to quietly dump in the group chat." She sniffed. "He makes your heart skitter, huh?"

I could hear the smile in her words. I put the K-Cup in my coffee maker and sighed as the liquid poured into the tumbler I'd placed under it. Deja knew me well enough to be able to tell when I was lying or trying to stall, but that didn't stop me from trying anyway.

"I wouldn't say all that."

"Don't play with me, Mon. You brought the man a hot chocolate. Voluntarily."

"So? It was a thank you for saving Treat Day. That's it. It's important to the residents." I grabbed the creamer and the sugar.

"So? That's basically a marriage proposal in your language. Did you thank him with your eyes too? Or maybe throw him a piece of ass to truly showcase your gratitude?"

"No!" I laughed. "It was just the hot chocolate. That's it."

"Fine. There's always next time. What's your plan?"

"My plan for what?"

"To move this thing forward! You two are stuck in the slowest of slow burns. I tell you what, after Treat Day, ask him to dinner."

I nearly choked on my coffee. "Me? Like a date?" I squeaked.

"No, like a work conference." She deadpanned. "Of course, like a date. It's time for you to see if these sparks are real or just journal induced."

I hesitated, "What if he says no?"

Deja laughed and then grew silent when I didn't join in. "Mon, he's been drooling over you since the cooking competition a few years ago. Are you seriously telling me you weren't aware of that? Stevie Wonder could see it."

"He's never said anything," I half-heartedly replied.

"You clearly weren't checking for him until the journal opened your eyes. Which is exactly why you need to go on an actual date with him. You need to see if the chemistry is real."

I hated how right she was. "You make it sound so easy."

"It is." she said. "You run into literal fires for a living, and you're scared of asking one man to dinner? I will personally drag you to The Hungry Hippo myself if you don't stop this self-doubt."

I laughed, despite feeling the nerves begin to bubble under the surface. "Fine. I'll ask him to dinner, but if this blows up in my face, I'm not speaking to you for at least a week."

"As if you could last that long. Deal."

We hung up the phone, a new resolve tucked deep inside of me. I needed to see for myself if whatever was brewing between us was real or if the journal had my vision clouded. I admit that I hadn't paid him much attention up until recently, but now that I had, it was hard imagining him any other way.

"You touch my marshmallow, and I will bite your hand, I mean it!" Birdie Mae hissed, "I've been saving my insulin for these!" The elderly man she was snapping at rolled his eyes and reached for another marshmallow from her plate. I chuckled as a popping sound followed. She had slapped him on the hand. We were knee deep in Christmas treats and the residents were enjoying themselves. Maybe a little too much. Some of them were amped up, reminiscent of small children who had been pumped full of too much sugar.

There were sticky fingers and sprinkles everywhere. I watched from the corner of the room as Pittman and Normil worked with a group of residents to frost a cake. Christmas carols played over the speakers in the room. The entire room was loud, warm, and festive but my gaze and attention kept sliding over to Jai.

He was surrounded by a group of women residents, sleeves rolled up and covered in flour. There was an ease in his wide smile that made it look like he belonged here. And maybe that was what caught my attention the most. He didn't look like he was performing or trying to show off or look good for anyone. He was just...him.

As if he could feel me staring, he glanced up and our eyes met. He held my gaze for a moment, something in his smile heating, before excusing himself from the crowd and making his way over to me.

"If I didn't know any better," he began when he was within earshot, "I'd say you were staring at me."

"No, of course not. I-" I glanced around, looking for something to use as an excuse. The half empty jar of candy canes was the only thing within reach. "I was going to ask you to save the candy canes before Ms. Birdie eats them all."

"Hey! Don't be involving me in your foolishness, little girl!" Her voice cut through the crowd and I flinched. For someone who was up there in age, her hearing was impressive. Jai raised an eyebrow, the corners of his mouth twitched like he wanted to smile but wouldn't.

"Right." He began, "Must have been imagining."

He turned, as if he were about to leave and I panicked. "Go out to dinner with me." I blurted and then threw a hand over my mouth when my brain finally caught up to what I'd said. He turned back to me and blinked.

"What?"

My heart stopped. Oh no, oh no, oh no. This is not what Deja had meant. "I-sorry. Forget it." I replied quickly, glancing around the room, hoping for the quickest exit. "What I meant was-um-never mind I just-"

He tilted his head and studied me. I could tell by the way he was looking at me so intensely that there was no way in hell he would let this slide. "Are you asking me out, Firefighter?"

I fumbled with the jar of candy canes in front of me, trying and failing to look casual. "No. I mean, yes, I am. If you want. It doesn't have to be a date though. We could just...hang out."

"Woof. This is hard to watch." Birdie Mae whispered. Jai shot her a quick look and then stepped closer to me.

"Monae." His voice was soft, gentle but there was something grounding in it that made my head snap up.

"Yes?"

"What do you call an old snowman?" he asked, stepping even closer.

I blinked, stunned by the question. "I- I'm not sure."

"Water." The way he stared at me so sincerely after telling one of the worst jokes I'd ever heard, made me throw my head back in shocked laughter. The tension and the awkwardness that had been building up, rolled off my shoulders.

"God, I cannot stand you." I laughed.

He grinned back. "You can tell me just how much over dinner tonight. What time am I picking you up?"

I stared at him, a little thrown off by how smoothly he took control of the situation and then turned my date invitation around on me. I was starting to see that charming side Audrey was so adamant about.

"Would seven work?"

"Girl, don't ask for permission!" Birdie Mae called from where she stood. "Tell him what time you'll be ready! He can adjust."

Jai rolled his eyes at her comment, but the smile on his lips told me that he didn't take offense.

"Seven thirty." I clarified. Birdie Mae nodded her approval and went back to her marshmallows and then narrowing her eyes angrily when she realized two had been stolen from her plate.

"Great." Jai replied, pulling my attention away from Ms. Birdie and back to him. "I'll be there."

I couldn't stop fidgeting with my napkin like a middle schooler on her first date. It was supposed to just be a dinner between friends after a long day of baking and eating treats with the residents of Whispering Pines, but I could not seem to relax.

"You good?" Jai asked, studying me. We were sitting in the back corner booth in one of my other favorite restaurants that wasn't Audrey's Kitchen or The Hungry Hippo. The last thing I needed was to have Audrey and Montrell watching us on this date. My nerves were already through the roof.

"I'm fine!" I protested a little too loudly. Jai said nothing, just gave me a look. I sighed. "Okay, maybe I am a little tense."

"Why?" His smile was slow and warm, but there was something serious tucked away in his expression that made my chest thump.

"This is too perfect. Too nice. What's the catch?"

"There is no catch," he said simply.

"That's what worries me!" I hissed, glancing around to make sure no one could hear us. I took a deep, steadying breath and forced myself to meet his gaze, even though the intensity was enough to turn my knees to jelly. "You're funny and charming. You're good with the residents at the nursing home and have the ability to negotiate like nobody I've ever seen. It's a lot to take in."

"So, what you're saying is," he tilted his head thoughtfully, "Is that you're looking for a flaw?"

"It'd be nice. I mean, something!" I shrugged.

He leaned forward, just a little. "I burn cookies."

Despite myself, I laughed. "Okay, fine but I'm serious! Most men hear what I do for a living and get weird about it. They don't like that I work long shifts or that I run into burning buildings on purpose or that I might be stronger than them. It creeps them out. Scares them off."

"Nothing about you scares me, Monae. I knew what you did for a living before I agreed to this date. You can't run me off that quickly."

I nodded and looked down at my plate, feeling embarrassed for being so vulnerable so soon. This was supposed to be a first date, the two of us getting to know each other outside of a work environment. But something about being near him made me want to bare my soul and it worried me because I wasn't sure if he felt the same way.

"It's hot, actually." A mischievous grin spread across his face.

I raised an eyebrow, "What is?"

"You. Your career. The strength and grace you exude. You've

captured my attention from the moment I first laid eyes on you."
He was smiling, but his gaze sent a shiver down my spine.

The rest of the meal passed in a blur of good food and even
better conversation. By the time Jai walked me to my car, my head
was a mess of contradictions. Fear and warmth and excitement
tangled together in my racing thoughts.

He reached for my hand and I let him take it, reveling in how
warm his skin felt to the touch. He held my hand for a moment
and then gently guided his fingers up my arm until he was cupping
my chin in his grasp.

He pulled me closer and then paused, glancing up to meet my
eyes in a silent question of consent. I nodded and held in a gasp
as his lips crashed into mine. A feverish dance of lips and tongues
tangling together. His arms snaked around my waist and pulled me
even closer.

For a moment, I allowed myself to get lost in his kiss. I allowed
my body to melt into his, just for a second, but then I pulled away
before I could do something reckless.

"Goodnight, Jai." I whispered, forcing a small smile.

He didn't look hurt or upset, just patient and determined.
"Goodnight, Monae."

The gentle way in which he said it, made me feel like this wasn't
over. Not by a long shot.

By the time I made it home, there was a journal entry waiting on
me. I wasn't surprised. I had half expected there to be something
here after Jai and I had such a good date. I placed my takeout tray in
the fridge, patted Blaze on the head and pulled the journal towards
me with a sigh.

DEAR DIARY,

IF SHE WAS HONEST WITH HERSELF, SHE WOULD ADMIT THAT SHE LIKES HIM. MORE THAN SHE REALIZED SHE WOULD AND THAT IS WHY DINNER RATTLED HER SO BADLY. THAT IS WHY SHE KEPT SEARCHING FOR THE EXIT, EVEN THOUGH THE NIGHT FELT SO SAFE.

HE ISN'T PERFECT, BUT HE'S STEADY WHEN SHE'S USED TO CHAOS. HE LISTENS AND HE MAKES HER LAUGH WHEN SHE'S BRACING FOR IMPACT. AND HE MAKES HER FEEL SEEN. SHE CAN CONTINUE TO RUN, IF SHE WANTS TO, BUT WHAT IF THIS TIME SHE STAYED? WHAT IF SHE GAVE IN TO THE DESIRE FOR SOMETHING, OR SOMEONE, STEADY? JAI DOESN'T SCARE EASILY, EVEN IF SHE DOES.

Chapter Seven

Jai

"So, you finally kissed her." Montrell said, after I filled him in on the date. Two days had passed, and I hadn't heard anything from Monae. I'd gone to the restaurant in hopes of distracting myself by making the schedule, but I'd been staring at the same empty excel sheet for the past hour.

"I did."

"So then why do you look like someone told you Christmas just got canceled?"

"It might as well have." I grumbled, placing my elbows on my knees and staring down at the floor. "I kissed her, and she kissed me back, but then she practically bolted. Said 'Goodnight Jai' and was gone before I realized what happened."

"And now?" he asked. He was chopping vegetables for the next shift. In the downtimes during staff switching over and moving from lunch to dinner, we would catch up on our days. I look forward to these moments, especially when our schedules are so packed that we don't get to hang out like we usually do. With me helping at the nursing home, I felt like it'd been a while since I'd been at the restaurant. Even though I was just here a few days ago.

"And now, nothing. Radio silence."

Montrell let out a low whistle and leaned over the counter, the vegetables momentarily forgotten. "What were you expecting? Her to profess her undying love and run off into the sunset with you?"

"It'd be nice." I muttered. He barked out a laugh and shook his head. "This isn't funny, Trell! I've been patient. I've shown up to every nursing home event, wore a dead man's Christmas sweater and-"

"What's this about a sweater?"

"Simon. It's Birdie Mae's late husband's sweater." I waved a hand, dismissing the rest of it, even though it looked like Montrell had more questions he wanted to ask. "Anyway, I've burned half the cookies in the city just to get her attention and then the one time she lets me in... she shuts the door in my face again."

"She's probably scared, man. She faces danger on a daily basis. She's used to being the one to handle things, she's probably not used to having someone willing to take the load."

"What do I even do with that?"

Montrell shrugged, "Keep showing up. Don't let her hide behind the tough-girl act. If you want her, make it clear you're not going anywhere."

The tension eased from my shoulders. "You make it sound so

easy."

"It's relatively simple. You're just dramatic."

I glared at him, but he just grinned and went back to chopping vegetables. As much as I hated to admit it, he was correct. I'd wasted so much time admiring from a distance. If I wanted anything to happen, I'd have to take control of the situation. In a sense, it was just like any other negotiation. And I wouldn't stop until we came to an agreement.

I'd never been inside a fire station. Until now. It smelled faintly of smoke and metal with a hint of cinnamon and coffee strong enough to wake the dead. Sean spotted me lingering by the entrance with a take-out bag from The Hungry Hippo and approached me, a knowing grin spreading across his face.

"I was wondering how long it would take you to grow big enough balls." He laughed.

"Have you seen Monae today?" I ignored his comment, nerves were already making me feel jittery. I wanted to see Monae and talk to her before I talked myself out of it.

"Yeah, she's in the bay. Don't touch anything unless you want her to hose you down." The goofy grin on his face did nothing to ease my nerves.

If I was honest with myself, I had lunch and no plan. No idea if she'd eaten already. No idea what I would say to follow up with my slightly impulsive gesture. No idea if she even liked the food that I brought. What I did know, however, was that kiss had been playing on a loop in my mind since it happened and I was tired of waiting for her to come around on her own.

I wandered in the direction of the bay, hoping to run into her before I saw any of her other coworkers. Boxes of tangled string lights next to piles of Christmas decorations littered the walk space. It looked like Christmas had stepped inside this fire station and threw up.

"Jai?" The sound of her voice made me freeze in my tracks. I turned, hoping I could come up with a good excuse before I saw her face, but I couldn't. Her hair was pulled back, exposing her cheekbones and the sleeves of her long sleeve t-shirt were rolled up at the elbows. There was a hint of a smile on her face as she tilted her head at me, examining the takeout bag and my sheepish expression. "What are you doing here?"

"I was in the neighborhood, and I thought I'd bring you lunch." I held the bag up to eye level.

Her eyebrows rose, "In the neighborhood? The Hungry Hippo is on the other side of town."

"Okay, fine," I smiled and shrugged, "I drove here on purpose. Since you seem to be dodging a nigga after our date the other night, I figured I'd come to you instead."

She blinked, surprised. I watched silently as her mouth opened like she wanted to argue and then closed again.

"I'm not here to force anything." I added, "I really did just want to bring you some food. Maybe even remind you that I meant everything I said the other night."

She glanced around, probably looking to see if anyone was listening, and jerked her head in the opposite direction. "Come.

Since you're here, you might as well sit down for a second."

I followed her through the station and into a small breakroom in the back. It smelled like leather and cinnamon. There were half finished mugs of coffee on the table. A few other firefighters milled around, shooting us curious looks as we passed.

"Okay," she said, gesturing to the table and leaning against the counter in front of it. "What are you really doing here?"

"I told you." I grinned, "I missed talking to you and I wanted to bring you some food."

Her eyes narrowed. "Jai..."

"Fine. I came to let you know that you can't just pretend that kiss after dinner didn't happen."

"Maybe I needed time to think about it." she shot back, folding her arms. "It's not like I work in a cute little office. My life is not that simple. People see a firefighter, and they think 'hero' or 'adrenaline junkie.' They don't see what comes with it: the hours, the calls in the middle of the night. The things you can't unsee."

I leaned forward, placing my elbows on the table. "Then let me see it."

She blinked at me, clearly not expecting that answer.

"I'm not saying it's not hard. I'm not saying you don't deal with a lot." I continued, "All I'm saying is that you don't scare me. Your job doesn't scare me. I know what it's like to be exhausted and to have people depending on you. Maybe not to the extent that you do, but I understand some of it. I don't want to be another person you have to protect. I want to be someone who stands in your world with you however I can. If you let me."

Something shifted in her expression. It was small, but it was enough to let me know that what I said hit something inside of her. She exhaled slowly and then took a seat in the chair across from me.

"I am starving. What did you bring?"

"Pasta." I replied, opening the takeout container. "Simple but effective."

"It smells amazing, I'm assuming you didn't make it."

Her comment made me burst out laughing.

"Are you ever going to let that go? I burn one batch of cookies!"

"First of all, it was three batches of cookies and second of all, no. I don't plan to." A genuine smile lit up her face while she teased me for the millionth time about the cookies, but I didn't mind the teasing. If that's what causes her to smile at me like that, I'd endure whatever ridicule she hurled my way.

We'd just settled into conversation, catching each other up on the mundane moments since we last spoke, when an alarm blared overhead. I flinched, the sound catching me off guard. Firefighters raced from all areas of the building, grabbing their gear and yelling to each other. Monae moved quicker than I'd ever seen her, sliding her chair back and scarfing down the last bite of her food.

"Duty calls." she shrugged.

"Go." I waved a hand, "I'll clean up before I leave."

She nodded. I'd already started grabbing the bowls and packing the rest of the takeout when I heard her voice from the doorway. "Jai?"

I looked up, "Yeah?"

"Don't get used to this."

I grinned. Couldn't help myself. "Way too late for that."

She rolled her eyes, but I could have sworn I saw a hint of a smile on her lips as she turned and raced to the truck. The lights were flashing and the alarms squealing angrily as it raced out of the bay and just like that, the building had gone silent again.

"Be safe." I whispered into the air, as the sounds of the sirens got quieter in the distance.

Chapter Eight
Monae

"Alright, so we have the decorator secured and the photographer said they'll get back with me about prices." Elodie marked things off her checklist, the bells attached to her Ugly Christmas Sweater, jingling with the movement. We had gathered in my apartment for a quick wedding planning moment. We still had a year to get everything settled, but Elodie and Mekhi were juggling multiple things at once. It would be the last year of high school for Kellan, their foster turned adopted son, and they wanted to focus as much on him applying and getting into his dream school.

"You're ahead of the game." Audrey remarked. "Trell says Mekhi has been obsessing over the song lists and securing the band."

"He has been. His standards are impossibly high since he plays professionally." Elodie rolled her eyes, but a smile spread across her face. "He's been calling in all of the favors with his musician friends so whatever he picks will be beautiful, I'm sure."

I listened as Elodie talked through the details she'd worked through so far. My mind wandered back to Jai. I wondered if he would be at the wedding. Mehki spent a lot of time at The Hungry Hippo, which meant he spent a lot of time around Jai, but I couldn't be sure.

"Is Jai invited?" I blurted before my brain could tell my mouth not to. Elodie paused, having been in the middle of talking about the cake, and tilted her head at me.

"Yes. Jai is invited. And even if he wasn't, I figured he'd be your date."

I blanched. "My date?"

Deja rolled her eyes. "Yes, Monae. Your date. Let's not pretend like you haven't been daydreaming about him ever since you kissed him the other-"

"Wait, hang on a second. Monae, you kissed him?" Audrey demanded. "And you didn't tell us?!"

"It wasn't serious." I sighed.

"That ain't what you told me."

"Deja." I glared at my friend. She grinned at me and shrugged.

"What? You keep doing this thing where you pretend you're made of steel and nothing phases you, but we know that's not true. You like him. You like him a lot, and it's scaring you. Admit it."

I looked down at my plate of snacks, wanting to deny it in protest, but I couldn't. She was right. Jai had been on my mind since I realized the journal was talking about him, but admitting that to myself felt like too much. Too vulnerable. Too open.

"So, Grandmada has been super excited for this Christmas dinner dance at Whispering Pines. It's all she's been able to talk about since Birdie Mae called with the invite." I flashed Elodie a grateful smile for the out her subject change had provided. She winked at me as she flopped on the couch next to me and snatched the remote out of my hand. I smirked at the nickname she uses for her Grandmother Amada, the originator of this journal. The staff at Whispering Pines and the team at Willow Glen thought it would be a good idea to open the final Christmas Event out to the public so the residents could invite family and friends if they wanted to.

"Hopefully people show up." I sighed. "It was a last-minute decision to open it up to everyone."

"Montrell and I will be there." Audrey called out from the kitchen, "Jai practically begged us to come."

At the mention of his name, my heart fluttered a bit. I shifted in my seat hoping to distract from the well of emotions I was feeling, but my girls knew me too well. Deja and Elodie narrowed their eyes at me and then glanced at each other, a barely suppressed smirk on both of their faces. I looked down into my cup, stirring the peppermint mocha for the millionth time, even though there wasn't a drop of whipped cream left.

Brina leaned forward and studied my facial expression. "You're brooding."

"What? I am not." I replied automatically.

"You've been stirring that cup like the answers will magically appear in front of you. Definition of brooding." Brina took on the professional tone she used at work when she was arguing cases in court. The same tone that let you know, she knew she was right and nothing you could say would change her mind.

Deja grinned. "We're all dying to know. Has the journal said anything else recently?"

I pulled the old book from where I'd been storing it in my bag and opened it to the last entry. I sat, shoulders tense, as each of them took turns reading the words. The last one to see it was Audrey and when she was done reading, she wordlessly closed the book and handed it to me.

"Well?" I demanded, looking at the four of them. "Out with it."

"Out with what?" Deja batted her long eyelashes in a fake attempt at being innocent.

"I know ya'll got something to say. Say it." I replied.

"Ask him to dance at the Christmas dinner."

"I'm not doing that." I replied automatically. ·

"If you don't, Birdie Mae will make it happen. She's been calling my grandma and updating her on the two of you since the first event." Elodie shrugged. "And you know she'll do it."

I shook my head. Birdie Mae would absolutely make it her mission to get me to dance with Jai. She had been entertaining herself with the two of us from the first day there. I felt like I could already see her gaze narrowing in on us while she plotted a way to put us together. If the journal didn't do it, Birdie Mae would somehow make it happen. Deja giggled, taking a sip of her own peppermint mocha.

"That entry is so cute. When it's my turn, I hope it gives me cutesy marketing puns."

"You're in the market for love..." Audrey chimed in, folding her hands under her chin and staring off dreamily into the distance.

The two of them collapsed in a fit of giggles when I tossed a pillow in their direction.

"Puns aside, it is very sweet. Jai has been interested in you for a while now." Brina reached for the journal again. "And it's even better because you are starting to finally notice him."

"Isn't that a bad thing though?" I asked. "Like, if he's so great why didn't I notice him before now? Isn't this clearly just the journal putting ideas in my head?"

The four of them laughed, seemingly all included in a joke I wasn't privy to.

"Girl..." Elodie gasped through her giggles.

"What?"

"Of course, you didn't notice him, honey." Audrey chimed in, placing a hand on my knee. "Your laser focus is one of the things that makes you excel at your job-"

"But it makes you terrible with everything else." Brina finished. "If it isn't in your already established priorities, it doesn't exist."

"You weren't looking for love, so of course, you'd have no reason to notice Jai."

"And that's why the journal had to practically shove him in your face with a cookie fire to finally get you to open your eyes." Elodie grinned and then clapped loudly. "It's a Hallmark movie in the making."

"What would it be called?" Brina asked.

We sat in silence, trying to come up with silly titles when Deja snapped her fingers. "I've got it!"

"Christmas by the Fire?" Audrey offered. Deja shook her head, her eyes lit up like the Christmas tree in the corner of my living room.

"A Smoky Little Christmas!"

I glared at her, but I couldn't stop the laugh that bubbled up.

I snapped the journal shut and tossed it on the bed like it had burned me. My stomach knotted so hard it stole my breath for a split second. A new entry had popped up after my girls had left and for some reason, this entry really got under my skin.

Anxiety tugged at my mind, making everything too big and too loud and too...much. Without thinking, I grabbed my keys and Blaze's leash. He hopped up after me, his tail wagging a mile a minute.

"Come on, Blazey. I need to go talk to someone really quick." He happily trudged behind me, excited to be going on a nighttime car ride. Those didn't happen very often. I glanced at the clock, worried it would be too late and I'd be turned away but I had to try.

When I arrived at the nursing home, it was in the middle of the shift change. I was able to sneak in behind one of the night nurses as she typed in the building code. I felt bad for being here after hours, but I was beginning to feel desperate, and I needed some words of wisdom.

The halls were quiet, lit with strings of colored lights. I found Birdie Mae sitting in the common room with a mug of steaming liquid, her hair tucked neatly into her fuchsia bonnet. All traces of makeup had been removed from her face, leaving her looking soft and fresh. She glanced up as I came in, confusion and then recognition flickering in her sharp gaze.

"Well, well, well. Look what the smoke alarm dragged in." Her mouth curved into that knowing grin that made me feel like I was ten years old. She patted the chair next to her. "What's got you out past curfew?"

I let out a heavy sigh as I approached. A crackly old Christmas song played on the vinyl record player to her left. I paused for a moment, enjoying hearing the familiar buttery voice of Nat King Cole, before taking a seat. There was a tightness in my chest.

"I just...needed to talk. If you're not busy."

Her gaze softened. "If you're here to tell me you've fallen madly in love with that restaurant man, you're too late. We have a running bet on when you two will get together."

"Birdie Mae!" I groaned, hiding my face in my hands.

"What?" She laughed, "The way he looks at you, it's a wonder the lights in this place don't blow a fuse."

"I kissed him the other night." I blurted. I could feel my cheeks heating as she remained silent, waiting for me to continue. "I ghosted him for a few days and then he showed up at the station to bring me lunch."

"And?"

"And... he makes me feel safe in a way I've never experienced before, and that terrifies me, because what if it's wrong? What if I let him in only to find out he can't handle me, my job, and the whole chaotic, unpredictable package that comes along with it?"

Birdie Mae studied me for a moment, before her expression relaxed into a gentle smile. "Your friend, Elodie. Did she tell you that I know her Grandmother?"

"Yes. She said you guys go way back."

"We do. We've been best friends all our lives. She listened to me countless times when it was my turn."

"Your turn?" .

"With the journal."

I sat up straighter, "Wait, you know about the journal?"

"Of course." She chuckled at my shocked expression. "That thing told me to stop ignoring the man who was right under my nose. Poor man waited for an entire year for me to come to my senses."

I blinked, stunned. "So, you wouldn't have been with him if not for the journal?"

"I probably would have taken much longer to figure it out. I was a stubborn lil girl. Always swore that men couldn't handle me and for the most part, I was correct. Until my Simon. That journal has a way of opening your eyes. Sometimes it shouts. Sometimes it whispers." Her warm hand found mine. Her grip was strong and steady. "If it's telling you to take the leap, then maybe you should listen. Life is too short to let the what ifs keep you from something good."

I swallowed the lump that was forming in my throat. "You make it sound so simple."

She gave me a knowing smile, "Love isn't always easy. But the good kind, the kind that lasts, is worth every ounce of courage it takes. And if there's one thing I know, it's that you my dear, have more than enough courage to see you through."

When I got back home, I dropped my keys on the counter and sighed. Blaze trudged over to his bed in the corner near the Christmas tree and flopped down like he had just worked overtime. His soft snores followed a minute later.

The journal sat on my bed waiting where I had left it. Birdie Mae's words echoed through my head for the millionth time since I left the nursing home. I flipped open the journal to the last entry that caused me to go running to Whispering Pines for comfort.

DEAR DIARY,

SHE'S STRONG ENOUGH TO FACE EXTERNAL ?RES, BUT NOT THE ?AME ?ICKERING INSIDE HER OWN CHEST. FEAR IS WHAT IS KEEPING HER FEET GROUNDED WHERE SHE STANDS, EVEN THOUGH HER HEART IS CALLING FOR THE MAN WITH THE CROOKED SMILE THAT PUTS HER AT EASE. HOW LONG WILL SHE CONTINUE TO BE AFRAID?

My stomach twisted. This entry felt less like an optimistic nudge and more accusatory. It felt like it was calling me out directly, questioning why I was so afraid. I put the journal down and grabbed my phone. I pulled up Jai's contact information, but my thumb hovered over the button to open a new message. I could text him. It didn't have to be something crazy; it could be a simple thank you for bringing me lunch at the station. Or, I could call him to hear his voice before I went to sleep, but my chest felt constricted, and my throat felt too full.

I could run full force into a building engulfed in flames, but when it came to running full force into a relationship, I cowered at the entryway. Men being intimidated by me and by my career had been my safety net, my security blanket. I didn't have to worry about getting my heart broken if they never stuck around long enough to get that deep.

This felt different. I locked my phone, tossed it on the bed, and then laid back with a groan. "Coward." I muttered at the ceiling.

As I drifted off into a fitful sleep, I imagined Birdie Mae shaking her head at me letting the fear take over once again, that knowing look of hers making me feel like I'd disappointed her somehow. Her words were still on a loop in my head: "Life is too short to let the what ifs keep you from something good."

But at the moment, here in my bedroom with no one to knock me off this negative hamster wheel I'd found my thoughts spinning on, the what ifs were winning the battle.

Chapter Nine
Monae

The Hungry Hippo had that warm, lived-in feeling tonight with soft light, a string of mismatched bulbs, and the smell of caramel and roasted coffee that made the whole place feel like a hug. Boyz II Men's "Let it Snow" played softly on the speakers. I grinned to myself as I looked around. Audrey had clearly gotten the better of Montrell on the decorating front; there was crooked tree in the corner, mistletoe over the kitchen pass, and tinsel tried valiantly to drape itself across the counter. Like someone found the decorations in the bargain bin at the last minute and knowing Montrell, that's probably exactly what happened.

I told myself I was just stopping by for a quick meal. The Hungry Hippo had the best burgers on this side of town, and I had decided I wanted one for dinner. It didn't even matter if Jai was here or not. A lie, of course. I found myself subconsciously scanning the room as I thought about the awful way I'd punked out and pulled back after our date. Even though I couldn't stop replaying that kiss that rewired my chest or the journal entries that kept nudging me forward. Everything I was trying not to feel even though it was the only thing I could think about.

He was sitting at one of the booths when I walked in, a blazer over his usual rolled-up sleeves, deep in conversation with a man in an expensive coat and a woman scribbling notes. His posture was confident, voice calm but firm, the complete opposite of the guy who once burned an entire tray of cookies in under six minutes. I paused near the counter, pretending to read the menu board while shamelessly eavesdropping.

"Community engagement isn't charity," Jai said, his tone smooth but sharp. "It's longevity. You get your logo on every flyer, every photo op, every social post from Whispering Pines about the Christmas events. That's months of goodwill attached to your name for a small contribution and a couple of your best holiday platters. Fair trade if you ask me."

The man leaned back, skeptical. "It's just not something we planned for this quarter. It's so last minute. Usually, these things are planned months in advance."

Jai didn't miss a beat. "Then make it a New Year's initiative. Start strong. Show people you care before your competitors remember they should. You know Jason would jump at the chance to get his foot in the door."

The woman at his side nodded slowly. The man exhaled through his nose. Then, just like that, broke out into a smile and extended his hand. "You know I can't stand that man or his horrible vegetables. Well played. You've got yourself a deal, Carter."

I blinked, stunned.

The man left smiling. Jai stayed seated, flipping through his notebook, calm and completely in control. I couldn't look away. Because the guy I remember fumbled his apron straps and told the world's worst Christmas joke. This one could probably sell snow to Santa.

As if he could feel me staring, Jai glanced up and the confident, cool businessman melted right back into the guy with the easy grin.

"Monae," he said, standing. "What are you doing here?"

"Grabbing a burger," I managed to mumble. "You were...busy."

He tilted his head. "You mean negotiating? You were listening, huh?"

"Maybe," I said, cheeks burning. "You're good at it."

His grin widened. "Don't sound so surprised."

"Were they a vendor?"

"Yes, a specific one that I only reached out to at the last minute. Birdie Mae told me they had the best sourdough bread, and I wanted to make sure she had some for the next few events."

I stepped towards the booth and slipped in across from him. He sat back down, smiling at me in the easy going way I was beginning to really enjoy. There was no showmanship. No grandstanding. Just a man who cared in a straightforward way, and it landed inside me like a warm ember.

Before I could say anything, Montrell stuck his head out of the kitchen. "Jai, distributor's here. Price doubled. You gotta talk to him before I do. These Christmas prices are insane." He nodded at me and then turned back to Jai; the irritation was rolling off of him in waves.

Jai rose. "On it." He strode to the door and took over the delivery situation with the same calm authority I'd just heard on the phone. I listened as he negotiated a discount, arranged a next-day fix, and got the guy to apologize. It was efficient; it was unflashy; it was everything I'd been telling myself I needed in a partner and then denying.

"Why do you still look so surprised?" he asked when he came back, there was a hint of a smile on his lips like he enjoyed the shock on my face.

"Impressed," I corrected. "Don't let it go to your head."

He grinned. "No promises."

The waitress sat the burger in front of me with a small smile and headed back to the kitchen. Jai studied me for a minute.

"Do I have something on my face?" I asked, wiping at my cheeks.

"You're perfect."

"You're so corny." I teased, even though I could feel myself growing warmer the longer he stared at me. "Want to join me?"

"I thought you'd never ask."

The next day, we were at Whispering Pines, setting up the room for the dinner and dance. I was starting to think of it as the Grand Finale of the Christmas events here at the nursing home, even though we had another event to get through before the dance.

Thankfully, the staff at the nursing home let us take over all of their extracurricular rooms so we had more than enough space to utilize. I think they were just happy seeing the residents finally excited about something. The community room had been transformed into one of those warm, small-town holiday scenes, twinkle lights, paper snowflakes, plaid table runners. Volunteers buzzed around like busy elves. Mrs. Raeford was fretting over centerpieces.

Somewhere between the hymns on a small speaker and Birdie Mae rearranging cookies for optimal festive effect, a coordinator flagged us down. "The layout is going to be an issue. One of the other firemen says the exit is partially blocked. Fire code inspectors could cite us." She threw a pointed glance in my direction.

My stomach did that tight thing. I'd spent years being the person who noticed exits, who watched for blocked pathways, who taught community groups the difference between cozy and unsafe. My first instinct was to step forward and fix it myself. No sweat, I had done it a million times out of habit, training, muscle memory. Except Jai didn't wait for me to move. Before I could open my mouth, he had sprung into action.

"Okay," he said, voice low but immediate, and he started organizing people like he'd done it his whole life. "We push these two tables back three feet. Leave that aisle clear. Volunteers, can one of you take down the extra chairs? Mrs. Raeford, can we relocate the gift table to the far wall?"

There was nothing theatrical about how he did it. No barking orders. Just small, clear directions that people obeyed because his calm carried them along. I found myself watching him, slightly off balance. He adjusted a table with one hand and then steadied an elderly volunteer's tray with the other. He listened when I suggested a line of sight for the emcee, integrated my input without flinching, and then stood back, taking in the room like a man making sure every piece fit.

"How'd I do, firefighter?" he asked, a smile on his lips.

"Amazing." I choked out, feeling an unexpected wave of emotions, I didn't know what to do with.

You, okay?" he asked when our eyes met.

"Yeah." My voice sounded small to my own ears. "I'm…You… you were paying attention to my inspections."

He shrugged, but there was a softness in his eyes. "You'd be surprised what I do when I care about something."

After the layout was safe and pleasant and exactly the sort of sensible holiday space that didn't make my teeth itch, the coordinator thanked him. Birdie Mae, never one to miss a beat, clapped Jai on the shoulder. "Carter, you got yourself some backbone tonight. Good for you."

He flashed that grin at her and then at me. "You're still staring."

"I'm not—" I tried to be dismissive, but my cheeks betrayed me.

He stepped closer, lowering his voice so only I could hear. "Listen. I'm not trying to push you into anything. I know you've got reasons for stepping back. But I want you to know something important, I'm not the person who runs when it gets hard. I'm not going anywhere."

Those words landed somewhere hot and dangerous in my chest. For once, they weren't a promise shouted in the dramatic, hurt way of past men; they were steady, present-tense, and something about their quietness made them harder to ignore.

We stood there in the warm glow of Whispering Pines, the smell of pine and cocoa curling around us, and a few residents happily singing a Christmas carol drifted in from the hallway. My walls, those bricks I'd built from fear and lessons and scars, felt like they shivered. Not a collapse just yet, but a dangerous loosening around the edges.

As I walked back to my car that night, the stars were brittle and bright. I had the journal in my bag, its pages still whispering the old push toward trust. But it wasn't the journal that felt different now. It was the knowledge that the man I kept imagining would run at the first siren was not Jai. I was comparing him to someone he wasn't, letting my past shape the way I viewed him.

I had watched him not only talk the talk but also quietly, calmly, take care of things when it mattered in my world. This wasn't the first time he had told me he wasn't scared to ride through the storms with me, but maybe, that notion was finally beginning to stick.

Chapter Ten

Jai

I was starting to enjoy spending time at Whispering Pines. I agreed to this as a way to be closer to Monae, but I was really going to miss some of the people here when the holiday season was officially over. My parents had been calling, bugging me to make a decision on whether I was coming home for Christmas morning in two weeks. I'd originally said no, but being around the residents and seeing the comradery amongst them, it was making me crave family time. Perfect opportunity to get some of my sister's famous pecan pie.

For a split second, I wondered what it would be like if I invited Monae back to my family's place. Considering how shifty she'd been since our kiss, that kind of gesture would send her running for the hills. Every time we made it one step closer, she'd stall and put more distance between us. It was frustrating, but I'd wait it out as long as it took.

Soft Christmas music played while the residents gathered in the common room for our next event. Christmas theater. We'd selected a few of the classic holiday movies for them to enjoy over steaming mugs of hot cocoa and peppermint tea for those who didn't like chocolate. The Christmas tree was completely covered in lights and ornaments the residents had created during the first event. There were barely any empty branches to be seen. The entire building was awash in Christmas decorations, a complete one eighty from the depressing ambiance this place gave off my first day here.

Birdie Mae was sitting next to one of the male residents whispering quietly, a thick blanket draping both of their shoulders. A few of the residents were coupled up while others sat with groups of friends or sat by themselves while Sean and one of the other firefighters set the movie up. We had a list of about five movies to entertain the bunch, but my guess is they would start falling asleep after the second movie. The room was dimly lit and cozy in a way that would make even the most hyper person settle down and feel drowsy.

Monae made her way through the groups of residents, smiling and greeting each person she passed. Her hair wasn't in its usual bun, instead it was hanging down around her shoulders in a beautiful twist out. The curls looked juicy and bouncy, and I had to resist the urge to run my hands through them. I appreciated the switch up. The soft red sweater and dark green jeans made her look festive but not like she was trying too hard.

She glanced up, catching me staring and something shifted in her expression when I didn't look away. After hiding my feelings for so long, I no longer had the energy to pretend like I didn't want to be around her. I was tired of pretending like I didn't want more from her than just one kiss outside of a restaurant.

The smell of burning peppermint snatched my attention. I whipped around towards the oven to see the peppermint and chocolate dessert I had been trying to make, turning into a lump of black goo. Montrell had told me not to push my luck. The last few events had gone well without me burning or ruining anything and I wanted to try my hand at this dessert I'd seen on Pinterest. The directions looked simple enough, but Montrell had warned me not to get too excited. I let the limited success get to my head. I was too cocky for my own good and now here we are...again. I turned the oven off and grabbed the pan. It wasn't until the searing pain settled into my fingers that I realized I had accidentally grabbed the pan without using an oven mitt.

I dropped the pan on the counter with a loud clang and then stuck my hand under cold water. The commotion caused a few of the residents to glance in my direction.

"Jai!" Birdie Mae called, "If you burn one more thing, I'm kicking you out of the kitchen!"

Normally, her playful jabs would have made me smile, but my hand throbbing in tune with my heartbeat distracted me.

"Do you need some help?" Her voice was soft, concerned and immediately reset my rapidly fraying nerves. I turned to find Monae watching me, an amused smile on her face as she surveyed the scene.

"I think it's beyond saving at this point." I threw a quick glance at the scorched baking sheet, my earlier enthusiasm for the Christmas Movie Marathon quickly dwindling. "Burned the hell out of my hand."

"Let me take a look." Before I could protest, she had crossed the room and grabbed my wrist, inspecting my angry red fingers. I tried to ignore the jolt my body felt at her touch. Her hands were warm, soft, and she smelled like a cinnamon cookie. "It's not that bad. Next time, use an oven mitt. That's what they're for."

When I didn't respond to her jab, she glanced up, concern on her face that quickly vanished when she saw how I was staring at her. I couldn't take my eyes off of her lips. I could feel her entire body tense up as she stared back at me. I closed the distance between us and gently placed my lips on hers.

The kiss started slow and timid like neither one of us wanted to step into it for fear of chasing the other away, but the longer our lips moved together the harder it was to contain myself. Her hand fell away from my wrist and slipped around my neck. The pain in my fingers barely registered against her sweater, as I pulled her body closer to mine.

"Jai." she gasped against my lips. Her voice was breathy and soft. All thoughts of Christmas treats, and nursing home residents evaporated from my mind under her touch. I wanted more. No—I needed more.

"Jai. Wait. We have to stop." Just as quickly as it started, she pulled away. Her chest was heaving, and her lips were puffy, and she never looked more beautiful to me than in that moment. I wanted desperately to take her somewhere and really show her how much I wanted this; how much I wanted her.

"What's wrong?" I asked.

"We can't."

"Right now? Or at all?"

She opened her mouth and then hesitated, avoiding my gaze like she was afraid I would be angry. I took a deep breath, trying and failing to stomp down the frustration that was bubbling in my chest.

"Do you have feelings for me, or am I just imagining all of this?" I demanded.

"Jai..."

"Answer my question." She flinched at the anger in my tone and then sighed.

"Of course, I have feelings for you! But I've told you before, I can't get involved just for you to leave when my job becomes too much."

"How about you let me decide what's too much for me to handle?" I replied. "We keep having this same conversation, what else do I have to do?" My frustration was growing at rapid speed. At this point, her treating me as if I was too fragile to handle what she did for a living was feeling disrespectful.

"I had a boyfriend once, a few years ago." She fidgeted with the buttons on her sweater. "He swore he was fine with the career I'd chosen."

I took a deep breath, feeling like a jerk for my earlier frustration. I knew she had reservations, but finally being able to hear why made her hesitation make so much more sense.

"You don't understand." she continued, tears gathering at the corners of her eyes, "I've been here before. I fell for someone who said all the right things. He said my job didn't bother him. Assured me that he loved how strong I was. And then one day, he just... left. Told me he couldn't handle always worrying, always wondering if I'd come home. Do you know what that did to me? To make myself smaller, softer, less...me and still not be enough?"

Tears slipped down her cheeks, making my heart feel like it was cracking in my chest. Without thinking, I reached up and swiped the tear that was falling down her face. I wanted to grab her and pull her into my arms. I wished I could go back in time and protect her from that hurt, but the only thing I could do in that moment was reiterate what I had been saying from the beginning.

"You don't have to be smaller with me. I like who you are and whoever you want to grow into being. The firefighter, the tough one, the one who looks danger in the eye and doesn't flinch. I'm not that guy, Monae. I don't scare easily, especially when it comes to you."

I grabbed her hand and brought it to my lips. She smiled faintly. "I'm sorry it's been so hard for me to trust that."

"I get it. I tell you what, let's just be here in the moment. I won't keep pushing you for something you're clearly not ready for, but that doesn't mean I don't want to be around you. We can just enjoy the night. Is that cool?"

"Yes." She flashed me a full grin this time, "I'd like that."

"You are absolutely out of your mind!" Monae shouted, the end of her sentence curling into laughter. The movies had ended, and the remaining residents had stuck around for a game of Uno that was quickly heating up. "You can't add a Draw 2 on a Draw 4!"

"I can," Birdie Mae deadpanned, slapping the cards down, "And I did. Your turn. Draw six cards, please."

I couldn't help but smile at the two of them. We were on the final round, everyone else had declared Uno and finished. Monae and Birdie were the last ones standing. Literally standing. The game had gotten so heated both women were standing and slapping their cards down on the table in a playful show of anger.

Bing Crosby sang softly in the background, about how he dreamed of a white Christmas. And for the first time this season, I could finally feel the magic of the Christmas holiday. My phone vibrated in my pocket, and I slid it out, thinking it was a message from Montrell hammering out final details for the Christmas dinner.

It was my sister, wondering if I planned to stop by her house at any point during the holiday. I sent her a quick reply, telling her that I would stop by on Christmas day, and slid the phone back in my pocket. When I looked up, Monae was watching me, a small smile on her lips.

"Are you distracting her?" Birdie Mae's voice cut through the tension that was rapidly filling the air. "Keep it up, so I can win this game."

"Not a chance." Monae bit back, still holding my gaze.

"You two are something else." I laughed. While the game finished up, I headed into the kitchen to clean up the last of my disaster, to minimize work for the nursing home cleaning staff. I had just finished wiping off the counters when Monae appeared by the door, looking like she wanted to say something but didn't know how.

"You good?" I asked, after a few moments of silence passed.

"Yeah. I just-" she sighed. "I just wanted to make sure you weren't upset with me. You know, after earlier."

"Why would I be mad, gorgeous?" I tossed the rag into the sink and leaned against the counter.

"Because I'm so...hesitant. I guess."

I studied her quietly for a minute, taking in her appearance. The sweater and the jeans that subtly hugged her curves. The soft curls brushing against her shoulders whenever she turned her head. She was art in human form, and I couldn't help but admire the masterpiece.

"I can understand that you need some time to trust that I mean what I say." I pushed off the counter and stepped closer to her. Her breath caught slightly at my movement, and I had to resist the urge to smile. Knowing I affected her as badly as she did me was oddly comforting.

"I'll give you your space, just know," I continued, leaning down so that my lips hovered just above hers, "I don't scare easily. Even if you do."

She closed her eyes and tilted her face even closer to mine, clearly giving me the okay for a kiss, but instead, I stayed still. When she opened her eyes and looked at me, I smiled.

"If you want me, you'll have to come get me yourself."

With that, I stepped around her and left the kitchen. Grinning to myself at the look of shock on her face.

Chapter Eleven

Monae

After the way he'd left me standing in the kitchen of the nursing home, with my lips puckered, waiting for him to kiss me, I've been kicking myself for not grabbing him right then and telling him I was ready. I wanted to be ready, but every time I tried to consider the idea, my body froze. None of it was his fault, it was all me. The idea of opening my heart to someone again made me want to pick up and run for the hills.

It was easier to run directly into a fire than it was to allow myself to be vulnerable with someone. I kept imagining myself the day my ex had dumped me, through text, after an incredibly hard shift. The day had started normally; the shift was running smoothly when we got the call. We'd had a fire break out in a home, and the father had lost his life making sure his wife and two kids got to safety. We'd tried everything we could to reach him, but the fire was too dangerous, even for our gear. These were the moments where I questioned whether or not it was worth it.

I'd practically crawled back to my bunk, bleary-eyed and depressed, to see the text waiting for me. I don't think I can do this anymore, Mon. I'm sorry. It's just too hard for me to have to worry about you every time you go to work. I hope you find someone who can handle it. I really do.

That moment had felt like someone kicking me when I was already down. After hearing the brokenhearted wails from the woman who had lost her husband and the children who had lost their father, all I'd wanted was to be able to crawl into someone's arms and sob. It wasn't his fault that he'd chosen the worst time to break up with me, how could he have known what type of call I was on? But that didn't change the fact that it stomped on what was left of my heart in that moment. It haunted me and impacted most of my relationship decisions afterwards. Because of his carelessness, I found myself unable to let go long enough to let a man I was really starting to like care about me. It wasn't fair to either of us, but I couldn't help it.

DEAR DIARY,

SOMETIMES THE BRAVEST THING YOU CAN DO ISN'T CHASING LOVE; IT'S STANDING STILL AND LETTING IT ?ND ITS WAY TO YOU. HE ?NALLY UNDERSTANDS NOW, THE WALLS BUILT, THE FEARS STITCHED INTO EVERY BRICK. HE KNOWS WHY IT HURTS WHEN SOMEONE GETS TOO CLOSE. AND STILL, HE STAYS.

HE SAID HE ISN'T LIKE THE ONE WHO LEFT. THAT HE DOESN'T SCARE EASILY, "EVEN IF YOU DO." AND MAYBE THAT'S THE DIFFERENCE THIS TIME. HE'S NOT HERE TO BREAK THROUGH ANY WALLS. HE'S HERE TO BE THE REMINDER THAT LOVE DOESN'T RUSH. IT REMEMBERS. IT RETURNS. IT WAITS. TRY AGAIN.

Frustrated tears slipped down my cheeks as I looked at this journal entry that was waiting for me when I got home. I felt angry with myself for being unable to relax enough to let Jai in. He hadn't done anything to disprove what he'd said to me, but I still held on to that fear. I reached for my phone and dialed her number, knowing she would cheer me up immediately.

"Girl," she says on the second ring, "Have you secured the man yet or nah?"

"Deja, I-"

"Oh Lord," she interrupted, "I can tell from your tone you're going to say no."

"It's not that simple!" I wailed, crying even harder.

"It never is," she said lightly, but then her voice softened. "So, talk to me. What's really going on?"

I exhaled, my chest tight. "You remember Marcus?"

Deja hummed. "The one who said he could 'handle dating a firefighter' and then dipped when he realized it meant you running into burning buildings while he watched Netflix? Yeah, I remember. Unfortunately. I never did like him."

I laughed a little, even though it hurt. "Yeah. Him."

"What about him?"

"I thought he was it," I admitted quietly. "I thought he and I would be married. He told me all the right things. Said he admired what I do, that it didn't intimidate him. And then one day, it was just... too much for him. He said he couldn't 'always worry about losing me.' And I—" the words caught in my throat. "I can't go through that again, Deja. I can't let someone get that close and then have them walk away because I'm too much."

There was a long pause on the other end, and I could practically hear Deja's smart remark fighting to get out before she swallowed it back.

"Monae," she said finally, softer than I've ever heard her, "you know what your problem is?"

I huffed. "No, but I'm sure you'll tell me."

"You think love is always supposed to feel safe."

That made me blink. "Excuse me?"

"You run into fires for a living, but you won't risk one in your heart," she said. "You want control. You want to know the floor won't give out. But baby, you're going to have to take the risk to get that reward. Circumstances are never perfect. Life can make love feel messy and unpredictable, but the right person won't be scared of that. He'll meet you in the middle of it."

I went quiet. The truth of it landed heavy, like smoke in the air.

"I'm scared, Deja."

"I know," she said. "But maybe it's time you stop asking if someone can handle your fire and start asking if you'll let them warm you up."

I laughed through the lump in my throat. "If I didn't feel so sad right now, I'd give you hell for that fire pun."

"It was right there; I had to go for it," she teased. "But seriously, Monae... don't push him away just because the last one couldn't keep up. Don't make him pay for someone else's mistakes."

"He said that if I wanted him, I had to come get him myself." I sniffed.

"Sounds like he's respecting your feelings while channeling his inner Silk Sonic and leaving the door open."

"Deja!" I whined, laughing.

"I'm just saying! You've been hot and cold with this man from the jump. He's probably protecting his peace at this point."

"So, what do I do?"

"First thing you do is come over and borrow this sparkly green dress, let me do your makeup and then you throw yourself at him during this Christmas dinner dance."

"What if that doesn't work? What if I pushed him away for too long?" I wiped my eyes and glanced over at the journal. It told me to try again. But, what if?

Deja snorted. "Girl please. He has been feigning for you since Montrell and Audrey got together. He isn't going anywhere. Trust."

After we hung up, I sighed and looked down at my phone. Blaze nudged my hand with his nose as if telling me to stop being scared and just do it. I rubbed his head as my other hand dialed the number before I could talk myself out of it.

"Hey, Firefighter." His voice was warm and smooth, like cinnamon over honey. "Everything okay?"

"Did I catch you at a bad time?"

"It's never a bad time to talk to you. I'm just getting everything ready for the next few days with us catering the dance and a few other events."

I smiled, even though he couldn't see me. "Sounds like you guys will be busy. I'll make sure I give you some space."

"I don't need space from you." He replied quickly. A lump

formed in my throat. Something in the tone of his voice hit me in the chest. "What are you up to? Busy avoiding me still?"

"I haven't been avoiding you." I lied.

"You have." His tone was light, non-accusatory, but there was something underneath his playful tone. Something that made my chest tighten even more.

"I um..." I sighed, the tension building in my shoulders, "I'm sorry for making things weird earlier."

"Things aren't weird," he said, gentle but sure. "At least not for me. I get it, Monae. You've been hurt before, and I might joke around too much sometimes, but I meant what I said—"

"What you said?"

"That I'm not scared of you. Or your job. Or the way you walk into a room like you already know you'll handle whatever happens. It's kind of what I—" He stopped, like he was deciding how much was too much to reveal. I found myself wanting to hear the words he was holding back. "It's what I like about you."

My heart started to thud in my chest, so loud I was sure he'd be able to hear it over the phone.

He continued, softer now, "You don't have to apologize for being strong. But you also don't have to pretend you don't need anyone, either. Not with me."

"You make it sound so simple."

He laughed. "It's not. It's frustrating. You throw me off my game sometimes."

It was my turn to laugh. "What? Me?"

"Yes, you. You're focused, disciplined, brave as hell. You walk into burning buildings, and I can barely make it through a catering gig without setting off the smoke alarm. But I like that about you. I like you." There was no teasing in his voice this time. Just steady honesty that wrapped around me like warmth from a fire I hadn't realized I was standing too close to. For a second, all I could hear was the quiet hum of the room and my own breath shaking on the exhale.

"I didn't mean to push you away," I finally whispered. "I just… I've been scared. Scared of how much I like you. Being vulnerable like this is terrifying for me. Dangerous situations I can handle, but this feels…worse somehow."

"I know," he said, "And it's not judgment. It's understanding. I've been waiting for you to stop running. And besides," he continued, his tone light again, "I'm pretty sure Birdie Mae and a few of the other residents are planning our wedding."

That made me laugh again, and the tension in my chest and shoulders loosened. The line went quiet again, and I pictured him sitting somewhere in that restaurant kitchen, maybe still wearing one of those ridiculous Santa aprons, leaning back in his chair with that half-smile that always gets me.

I want to say something witty, something to lighten the weight in my chest, but instead what comes out is, "I'll see you at the Christmas dinner, right?"

"Wouldn't miss it for the world," he said, the smile in his voice evident. "And Monae?"

"Yeah?"

"I'll save you a dance. Unless you're too busy saving the day again."

I laugh this time. Soft, real, unguarded. "I'll try to pencil you in."

"Good," he said, voice low. "Because I'm done letting you slip away."

When we hung up, I sat there for a long time, staring at the glowing Christmas lights and decorations strung all around my living room. My chest felt light and heavy at the same time, but for once, the feeling didn't scare me. I don't know what it was about that conversation, but I'm glad I'd decided to call him. He was understanding of my hesitation, but still intentional with me.

If I was honest with myself, I'd already developed feelings. Each burned dessert and kitchen disaster pushed me one step closer to him. I was already hopelessly gone and we'd only been on one date. We'd kissed a few times, sure, but what really tossed me over the edge was seeing how he could take charge in his own areas of genius. He and I were alike in that way. Maybe I couldn't trust him to make the food, but could I trust him with my heart? When I had a dangerous call or back-to-back schedules, would he still feel the same about me?

For the first time, I wasn't scared of the answer. I'd been running from this feeling for so long, but maybe I was supposed to be running towards it.

Chapter Twelve
Monae

"Are you sure this isn't too much?" I asked, staring at myself in my full-length mirror. Deja had come over with makeup, garment bags, and hair pins, insisting I put on her green sequin mermaid evening dress with the slit that climbed the thigh and the delicate strands of jeweled chains that draped down over the shoulders like sleeves.

The neckline dipped just enough to tease, but not enough to give too much away. The entire gown shimmered like a constellation come to life, the deep emerald velvet and the gold sequins caught every flicker of light as I turned to get a good look at myself from all angles. I had hesitated at first, wanting something a little simpler, but I couldn't deny how good it looked on my body.

Deja stood behind me, finger on her chin, staring me up and down with hawk-like precision. "If it goes the way I am thinking, these residents are going to pull out all the stops with their attire.

You have to step like you know how to handle yourself."

"Yeah, but I feel like a Christmas ornament." I whined.

"Good." she replied, "Blind him with your beauty."

I sighed in resignation as she pulled out her makeup kit to get started on my look. I wanted to tell her not to do too much on the eyes, but this was Deja. Being extra was her comfort zone. By the time she got finished with me, I would look like I was going to the Oscars and not a nursing home for a Christmas dinner dance.

"You keep fidgeting like that, and you're going to end up looking like the Joker. Is that what you want?" she warned, holding a blending brush in one hand and an eyeshadow palette in the other. "Why so serioussss?"

"I'm not fidgeting," I said automatically, ignoring her terrible Joker impression, then immediately adjusted the neckline of my dress for the fourth time.

Deja arched a brow. "My girl, the firefighter who's run into actual flames without flinching, is nervous about one dinner dance?"

"It's not the dance," I said. "It's… everything. The journal. Jai. The way he looks at me like I hung the Christmas lights and the moon at the same time. It's too much."

Deja grinned, stepping closer. "You know, most people would kill for a man who looks at them like that. You get one and suddenly you're allergic to happiness."

"I just—" I sighed, closing my eyes so she could continue blending. "I really like him, Deja. Like, really like him. And that's what scares me. Because the last time I liked someone this much, it ended with me second-guessing everything about myself."

Deja softened, setting the blending brush down and narrowing her eyes at me. "He's not Marcus."

"I know he's not." I replied, "But this all feels so familiar. Too familiar. It makes me want to run away from it all."

"Maybe on the surface level it's familiar, but you've never been with Jai before."

"I know, I know," I said quietly. "Part of me feels like this could be it. Like he could be it. It's why I keep holding back with him. Because if he changes his mind, if he decides I'm too much again, I don't know if I could bounce back from that."

"Again? Listen to yourself, Mon. You're moving as if he's already hurt you, without giving him the chance to prove that he won't." Deja studied me for a moment, her eyes sharp but kind. "You know what I think?"

"I'm almost afraid to ask."

"I think you're overthinking yourself right out of a happy ending."

I groaned. "That's your sage advice?"

"Oh, there's more," she said, grabbing her brushes and getting back to work. "You're used to saving people, Monae. It's what you do. But this time, you don't have to. You just have to let yourself be the one who's loved. That's the brave thing here. Not fighting fires, not being tough. Just… being open."

I swallowed hard. "What if it doesn't work out?"

"It might not. But, what if it does? You owe it to yourself to at least try. If anyone deserves something good, it's you."

Her tone was softer now, all sarcasm stripped away. She picked up a pair of sparkly earrings and handed them to me. "Now, put these on and go show that man why he hasn't stopped smiling since the day you met him."

I laughed, blinking back the sudden sting in my eyes. "You're ridiculous."

"Ridiculously wise, thank you very much."

The quiet rustling in the corner caught both of our attention. The journal was flipping its pages, as if it wanted to chime in on the conversation. I glanced over at Deja who was watching the journal with an odd expression. Blaze, who had become accustomed to the noise the journal made, snored happily on his back in my bed, his feet pointed in the air and his mouth open in a lazy grin.

It took a few minutes, but when it finally stopped flipping the pages and settled down, Deja nodded at me.

"Go see what it says," she whispered.

DEAR DIARY,

SOMETIMES THE HEART ALREADY KNOWS WHAT IT WANTS AND IT JUST WAITS FOR COURAGE TO CATCH UP.

SHE'S STOOD IN FRONT OF DANGER WITHOUT FEAR, BUT LOVE HAS ALWAYS FELT LIKE A DIFFERENT KIND OF ?RE. ONE SHE COULDN'T CONTROL. ONE SHE WASN'T SURE SHE COULD SURVIVE.

BUT NOT ALL ?AMES ARE MEANT TO DESTROY. SOME ARE MEANT TO WARM, TO LIGHT THE PATH FORWARD, TO REMIND HER THAT SHE'S STILL CAPABLE OF BEING SOFT AND BRAVE AT THE SAME TIME.

HE'S BEEN STEADY, PATIENT, WAITING FOR HER TO SEE THAT HE WAS NEVER RUNNING TOWARD HER FIRE TO TAME IT, ONLY TO STAND BESIDE IT. TO STAND WITH HER IN IT. NOW IT'S HER TURN TO STEP FORWARD. TO TAKE THE LEAP. TO LET HER HEART ?ND ITS MATCH IN THE GLOW THAT'S BEEN WAITING FOR HER ALL

ALONG.

I looked up, eyes misty, after reading the entry out loud. The smile on Deja's face was so bright, you'd think the message was written to her. A sense of peace settled in my chest. Even though I couldn't predict what happened next, choosing to take that step with him felt like the right decision.

"You heard what it said," she giggled, "Go get your man, girl."

Whispering Pines had really thrown out all the stops for this dinner dance. I'd pulled Deja in for her connects in the decorating industry and she put me in touch with a decorator that came highly recommended. The fire chief had mentioned the budget for this event would be no object, because he'd wanted to make sure his mother got the best holiday celebration we could manage. He had been willing to cover the extra costs to make sure everything was just as good as it'd be if she'd planned it herself.

The moment I stepped into the Whispering Pines common room turned ballroom, I felt the magic. String lights draped across the ceiling like golden constellations. The Christmas trees we had decorated earlier glowed under the lighting, the sparkly ornaments twinkling each time the light touched them. Paper snowflakes fluttered from the vents every few minutes, and the smell of cinnamon, nutmeg, and baked apples wrapped around me like a hug. It felt like I had stepped into a movie scene and I couldn't help but smile.

After meeting the residents here at Whispering Pines, seeing how drab and lifeless everything was at the start of all this, I felt proud that we were able to turn it around. Everyone deserves a magical Christmas. I was grateful for my friends being willing to step in and help put this entire thing together. I caught a glimpse of Audrey and Montrell in the kitchen laughing while they finished the last bits of the meal, they'd been more than willing to cater for tonight.

Residents in festive sweaters filled the room, laughing, swaying, and showing off their Christmas bling. I'd thought that my dress would be too much, but Deja was right. Everyone had pulled out their best outfits for tonight. I wasn't the only one covered head to toe in sequins. Birdie Mae was holding court near the buffet table in her sequined cardigan, already scolding someone for eating the gingerbread centerpiece. Her outfit shimmered every time she moved her arms. I smoothed my hands down the front of my dress and scanned the room for him.

And there he was.

Jai Carter, in a green suit that matched my dress with an open burgundy shirt underneath, adjusting a tray on the dessert table. The suit was expertly tailored and fit him well enough to show off those shoulders and make my pulse jump. It blew my mind how I'd never noticed him before. I was unable to look away now, completely caught up in his vibe. He carried himself with such a quiet confidence, even when he was being silly or ruining a dessert, he moved with a self-assurance that captivated me. He looked up at that exact moment, and our eyes met across the room.

My heart stuttered.

His lips curved into that easy smile, the one that always made me feel like the only person in the room. He murmured something to Birdie Mae, who grinned and gave him a shove in my direction.

I didn't move. Not right away. My feet felt glued to the floor, my mind racing with all the reasons I should be careful, should keep my distance, should protect the fragile balance we'd built. I glanced at the exit, suddenly feeling like I needed to turn and make a run for it.

But then I remembered the journal.

Now it's her turn to step forward.

And just like that, I did.

Jai met me halfway, his eyes warm and searching. "You made it."

"I told you I would," I said, pretending my voice wasn't shaking.

"I wasn't sure. Thought maybe I'd have to start another fire just to get your attention."

I laughed, the sound slipping out easier than I expected. "Please don't. I'm off duty tonight."

"Good," he said softly. "Because I'd really rather dance with you than get sprayed with a fire extinguisher."

He held out his hand. For a heartbeat, I just stared at it, broad, steady, waiting. Then I took it.

His hand was warm against mine as he led me onto the dance floor. The music started playing something slow and classic, Nat King Cole, and suddenly it felt like the whole world had gone quiet except for the two of us.

"You look beautiful," he said, voice low.

"Thank you. You clean up nice." I replied, making a point to admire his outfit. The fit of the suit, the colors that blended together to give the perfect holiday vibe without doing too much. "Did you know I was wearing green?"

"Your friend Deja told Audrey what color your dress was and Audrey told me." He smiled. I glanced over his shoulder just in time to see Audrey wave enthusiastically and give me a thumbs up. Montrell shook his head, but I could see him fighting back a smile of his own.

"That figures." I laughed, but then quickly turned serious. "Can we find somewhere to talk?"

Jai pulled my hand up to his lips and planted a soft kiss on the back of it, "We absolutely can. I just need a few minutes to make sure everything is set up. Birdie Mae's son is here, and I've been told he is big business."

"Wait- Chief Lillard is Birdie Mae's son?" The realization clicked as soon as he said the words. They looked so much alike, I couldn't believe I hadn't put it together sooner. I scanned the room for her, finding her standing with the Chief, fussing over his tie. Seeing the large, usually no-nonsense man bending down so the tiny woman could fix his tie was enough to make me shake my head.

"Give me twenty minutes and then I'm all yours." Jai's voice brought me back to the present moment. I nodded, and he gave me a slow once-over, shaking his head with a low, appreciative whistle before backing away and jogging to the kitchen. I took the moment of reprieve as a chance to go speak to Birdie.

"Well, don't you look absolutely stunning." She gushed when I was within earshot. "Give us a spin, darling."

I obliged, spinning slowly so she could get a good look at the entire dress. She tutted in appreciation.

"I see why that boy drools over you so much, all that booty you got back there!"

"Mom!" Chief Lillard admonished. She waved a dismissive hand in his direction and grinned.

"So, is tonight the night?" She asked, wiggling her perfectly manicured eyebrows. I threw a quick glance at Jai, he was in the kitchen talking with Montrell, a serious expression on his face.

"Yeah," I replied, trying not to sound as dreamy as I felt. "I think tonight is the night."

"Perfect! Look, if you two need a moment of privacy, there is a storage closet down the hall and around the corner that only the day shift uses, you can-"

"Mom! You can't be serious." Chief hissed.

"Hush, boy!" she snapped playfully. "You in women's business. Now, as I was saying..." She grabbed my arm and pulled me away from where the Chief stood. He watched us, eyes narrowed, but I could see the hint of a smile on his lips. Even though he was trying hard to hide it.

"There is a storage closet down the hall and to your right. It's usually unlocked because the second shift staff is always too distracted to lock it. Take him in there if you two need a moment of privacy. Give me the nod and I'll stand guard."

I laughed, not at all shocked by her shenanigans anymore. "You don't have to do that, but thank you."

"Just offering my assistance." She shrugged. "Until Amada gets here, I have nothing interesting to do."

My ears perked up at the mention of Elodie's grandmother. "Ms. Amada is coming tonight? I didn't know that."

"We were allowed to invite a guest, and other than you two and that old goof over there," she pointed to the elderly gentleman trying and failing to sneak cookies from the table, "I don't really talk to anyone else."

"I think you need to go grab him," I replied. "If not, there won't be any cookies left for the rest of us."

She shook her head. "If you are what you eat, he ain't nothing but a big ole box of chocolate chip." Squeezing my hand, she continued, "Good luck tonight, even though you won't need it. He is completely smitten with you."

I squeezed her hand in return, "Thank you."

With a small smile, she turned on her heel and hurried over to the table. "Gerald! Put those down, for Christ's sake, you can't eat every cookie in this building!"

"Dance with me." His voice was soft, and right next to my ear. It sent shivers down my spine. I turned to face him, resisting the urge to throw my arms around his neck and shove my tongue down his throat instead.

"Okay." He offered me his hand and led me to the middle of the dance floor. We were the only two out here, everyone else was gathering around the food tables or talking amongst themselves off to the sides, but it didn't even matter.

"Did I tell you how beautiful you look tonight?" he asked.

I nodded. "Couldn't hurt to hear it again though."

"You possess the beauty that musicians write songs about. I

haven't been ,ole to concentrate since you walked in."

"Wow." ,aughed, "That was poetic."

"I'r ,nan of many talents." He smiled back as we swayed gently , music. "So, have you thought any more about what we've ,ed about?"

"Yes, I have."

"And?"

"I want..." I swallowed, suddenly nervous. He waited, even though I could feel his body tense, "I want...you. I want to be with you. I want to give us a real shot."

I could barely get the words out before his lips crashed into mine and his arms wrapped around me.

"You have no idea how long I've been waiting to hear that." He breathed. "As soon as this dance is over, I want to take you somewhere. Just you and me."

"Actually," I replied, a slow smile spreading across my face, "Do you want to get out of here for a second? Go somewhere more private?"

His eyebrows rose, but he nodded. "Lead the way."

The laughter and chatter of the residents faded behind me as Jai's hand found mine. He didn't say a word as I led him past Birdie Mae waving cheerfully at the staff and a few of my coworkers, and into the quiet hallway. My pulse thundered in my ears, but I couldn't pull away from him.

"Are you sure about this?" he whispered as we slipped into the storage room, the door clicking softly behind us. He was smiling, that lazy, confident grin that made my stomach twist.

"I've never been more sure." I whispered back.

The room smelled faintly of pine-scented cleaning su~~lies and~~ leftover decorations, but all I could notice was him, the ~~nth~~ radiating from his body, the heat in his eyes.

Before I could stop myself, he was pulling me close. His hand cupped my face, thumb brushing over my cheek in the slowest, most deliberate motion. My knees nearly gave out, and my body began to heat.

"I've wanted this," he murmured, voice low and rough with something I couldn't name. Desire, need, longing, all of it wrapped together. "You... you have no idea how much."

I swallowed hard, my hands finding his chest, feeling the steady thrum of his heartbeat. "Jai..." I began, then stopped, feeling too emotional to be able to form my thoughts into words.

"Shh," he whispered, pressing his forehead to mine. "Not yet. Just let me be here with you."

I let the world slip away, the dance, the decorations, the watchful eyes of Whispering Pines, until there was nothing but his warmth and the ache of finally being able to let myself lean in.

His lips brushed mine, tentative at first, teasing, exploring, and then firmer, hungrier, like all the moments we'd held back exploded at once. I pressed closer, wrapping my arms around him, feeling him respond instantly, his hands moving over my back, pulling me flush against him.

The storage room's dim light caught the shimmer of my dress and the glint in his eyes, and for a moment, I thought I might combust right there. The air between us was thick, hot, and dangerous, but I didn't care.

"God, Monae," he breathed against my lips, and it was all I could do not to let go completely, not to fall into this fire I'd been avoiding for so long. "Can I?" he asked, letting his hands travel further and further down my body until he reached the beginning of the slit in the dress. His fingers only grazed my bare skin, but the shock of it made my breath catch in my throat.

I nodded, unable to form words, as he placed his lips softly on mine again. He pulled my leg up around his hip and slipped a finger past my panties. The low, guttural groan that escaped his lips when he slipped a finger inside me was enough to send me into a frenzy.

"You're so wet." he groaned, exploring me with his fingers. "Is this for me? This mine?"

"Yes." I breathed, gasping a little as he pushed another finger inside of me. He kissed me again, hot and hungry, nipping softly at my lips. I moved my hips against his hand, desperate for more. I needed more. He wrapped an arm around my waist and hoisted me up, so I was sitting on the stack of chairs in the corner of the closet and propped my heel on the shelf with the cleaning supplies. He stepped back and studied me for a moment with a low whistle. I was open and exposed to him, but instead of feeling scared of the vulnerability, I'd never felt safer.

"The reality of you is even better than the dream, you know that?"

"Jai..." I whimpered.

"I mean it." he whispered, dropping to his knees. It took everything in me not to cry out as he plunged a finger deep into my wetness. It had been so long since I'd had anyone's fingers but my own inside me and the sensation was almost too much to process in the best way. My vision blurred as he gently slipped my panties down my legs and stuffed them in his pocket. Before I could get my thoughts straight, he put my other leg over his shoulder and replaced his finger with his tongue.

I gripped the sides of the chair and clamped my teeth down on my lips so I wouldn't scream in this closet and ruin the entire thing. His lips and tongue moved with such skill and precision I could feel myself reaching the brink and tumbling over.

I felt my walls crumble, piece by piece, as he pressed closer, as he whispered my name like it was sacred and the distance between us vanished. I wanted this. Wanted him. Needed him. Every fear, every doubt melted in the heat of his hands, his lips, his gaze. His touch.

And when the door creaked faintly, reminding me that we were still in Whispering Pines, I didn't pull away. I couldn't. I just shifted my hips, letting his tongue deepen and his fingers slip in and out of me while the pressure began to build again and again. When I felt myself coming apart once again, I put my hand under his chin and guided him back up to my lips. Tasting myself on his tongue. When I came against his hand, he covered my mouth with his free hand, his eyes wild and full of want as he watched me break apart again beneath him. Finally letting the unspoken promise of everything waiting outside the door hang thick between us.

When we finally broke apart, breaths mingling, eyes locked, I felt it in every fiber of me: the spark had ignited, the barrier gone, and there was no turning back.

"I've wanted you forever," he murmured, voice low, intoxicating.

"I—" I tried to answer, but words failed me.

Instead, I pressed my forehead to his again, letting the heat and

Chapter Thirteen
Monae
10 Months Later

"Trick or treat!" the group of children hollered as soon as I came to the front desk of the fire station. We were doing the community Trunk or Treat here at Willow Glen and I was having the best time looking at all of the cute costumes children and their parents were coming up with.

"You guys look great! Candy is that way!" I pointed to my left and laughed as they made a beeline for the candy set-up. This was literally the last moment of peace I'd have before we hopped into wedding mode full swing. Elodie was getting married this Christmas season and we were shoving the bachelorette weekend, bridal shower, and wedding all in these next few months. I looked down at my Mrs. Incredible costume and smiled. As much as I loved Christmas, Halloween was always my favorite. It was a chance longingdresakufofdrothights.

"Tonight, 'hclthingashdinravoiced and the low whistle of approval that followed made my smile deepen. I turned, to find Jai dressed as Mr. Incredible, holding a plastic pumpkin full of candy. "That is so unfair."

"What is?"

"Seeing the way, you fill out that costume and not being able to take you home and-"

"Trick or treat!" Another group of children filed in, interrupting whatever horny comment Jai was about to make. He shifted the pumpkin to the front of his costume and turned away from the kids, awkwardly.

I laughed and jerked a thumb over my shoulder, "Follow the music."

Oblivious to his struggle, the children ignored Jai and went running towards the fun. He sighed and turned back to me.

"I feel like you did this on purpose." he grumbled, rolling his eyes at me.

"I haven't done anything. I'm just here in my costume."

"But when you look this good, how can you expect me not to stare?" After last Christmas season, and the dinner dance at Whispering Pines, Jai and I had been inseparable. Whenever I wasn't working, we were spending time together. And even when I was working, he would come by the station and bring dinner for the crew. His cooking skills had exponentially improved since we started dating.

So far, he has proven true to his word. During the tough calls, he was always there to listen to me vent or to hold me while I cried. He never flinched, he never wavered, and he never once made me feel like I was too much. I'd fallen hopelessly in love with this man, and he was just as crazy about me.

"Come here." I hooked my finger in his direction, beckoning him closer. As soon as he was within arm's reach, I threw my arms around his neck and kissed him. The plastic pumpkin he'd been holding clattered to the floor, spilling candy everywhere. I pulled away to grab the candy, but he pulled me in closer and continued to kiss me. I obliged, laughing against his lips.

"Get a room, you guys!" Sean called, making fake gagging sounds as he walked past. The cape on his Captain America outfit fluttered behind him dramatically.

Jai didn't respond, just tossed up a middle finger and continued to press his lips against mine. Even after being together for almost a year, he could never get enough of me and if I'm honest, it felt good being with a man that never tired of my touch or my kiss.

"Okay. Okay wait." I giggled in between kisses. "We do need to cool off. There are kids here."

"Forget them kids."

"Jai!" I laughed.

"Alright, fine. Sorry, but tonight I want my time with you."

"With or without the costume?"

He turned to look at me and I twirled to give him a full view. "Keep it on."

He was insatiable. And so was I.

Local businesses had partnered with us to help bring a safe

Halloween to the community. Some parents didn't feel comfortable letting their kids wander the streets begging for candy from strangers. Our Trunk or Treat offered them a safe alternative. The Hungry Hippo, Audrey's Kitchen, and a few other restaurants in town had partnered with us to bring treats and good food so the parents had something to enjoy while the kids had fun and played games.

Community events were a big reason why I loved my job so much. All of the hard calls we had, didn't compare to the moments we could give back to the community. After the success of working with Whispering Pines last year, they'd asked the station to come back and do another Christmas event with them.

I was more than happy to be in charge of the event this time. It gave me the excuse to go back and spend more time with Birdie Mae, who was becoming more and more like my own grandmother figure. She offered advice, sometimes unsolicited, and I would visit her room to trade fashion secrets and catch up on her stories with her.

She was quickly becoming one of my favorite people. When Jai had time, he would come with me. Watching the two of them bicker and fuss like mother and son always made me smile. Last year when we began working with Whispering Pines, I had no idea she would become such a big part of my life.

A quiet rustling from under the front desk caught my attention. The journal had been suspiciously silent over these last ten months, but I'd had the feeling that I would be hearing from it sometime soon, so I kept it with me. I smiled to myself as I reached down and peeked at the journal in the drawer where it rested.

The entries that had encouraged me to give Jai a chance were disappearing right before my eyes. Even though our story was just beginning in real life, I felt a tiny wave of sadness seeing the words that had given me the courage to take the leap vanish right in front of me. I no longer needed the guidance it offered.

"What is that noise?" Jai asked, coming to stand behind me. I didn't reply, just kept watching the journal do its thing. As my story erased, it prepared itself for the next story that I knew was coming. One I personally couldn't wait for.

THIS JOURNAL BELONGS TO DEJA JOHNSON

About The Author

Lauren Roach is a dog obsessed, true-crime loving, self-proclaimed book nerd that has always dreamed of becoming a published author. While most kids were frolicking in the sun, Lauren chose the path less sweaty and opted for the cool embrace of air conditioning while immersed in a book or busily penning fan fictions about whatever heartthrob boy band was on her radar.

Lauren's literary ambitions took a brief hiatus when she decided to venture into the world of criminal justice, earning both a bachelor's and a master's degree in the field. Even though she has yet to use either one of her degrees for anything career-related, she hopes to maybe use her criminal justice knowledge to one day write a really good mystery plot.

Fast forward to today, Lauren is happily residing in North Carolina with her lovely husband where she records episodes for her book centered podcast Lauren's Library and isn't afraid to break out a book in the middle of a social gathering. You can follow her work at

Instagram & Threads: @thebookybabe_
Tik Tok: @thebookybabe
Podcast: Lauren's Library Podcast
Website: www.sunflowerrosepublishing.com